A TRAP FOR AN INNOCENT

A TRAP FOR AN INNOCENT

Hanna-Kaarina Hadkinson

Devon Libraries

Book Guild Publishing
Sussex, England

First published in Great Britain in 2007 by
The Book Guild Ltd
Pavilion View
19 New Road
Brighton
BN1 1UF

Typesetting in Baskerville by
IML Typographers, Birkenhead, Merseyside

Printed in Great Britain by
CPI Antony Rowe

A catalogue record for this book is available from
The British Library.

ISBN 978 1 84624 173 4

1

Tina, a blue-eyed blonde, grew up in an idyllic setting, a dairy farm in Finland, in the south-west of the country. The homestead was surrounded by fields and woodland, dense with tall, straight fir trees, often referred to as 'green gold'. You couldn't see any neighbours, as the nearest farm was almost a kilometre away. The year was 1941, when Tina was born into a family of one set of grandparents on her mother's side, a sister and brother, who were two and a half years old and twins. And of course there was mama, twenty-seven years of age at the time. Her father, an army officer, was on active front-line duty at the Russian border. When she was three weeks old, Tina's father was killed at the front, and her mama's auburn hair turned silver grey overnight from the shock.

So, Tina never saw her father, except a framed photograph on the wall. A gold fob watch was returned from the battlefield, its glass shattered in a grenade explosion. So little left of the handsome soldier, who departed so suddenly, at the age of thirty-two, having never seen baby Tina.

Within that same year, both grandparents passed away peacefully, having never suffered any major ailments. Most of the able-bodied men were fighting in the war, so the running of farms was left to the women and children. Neighbouring farmers gave a helping hand to one another. Also, there was Kirsty, who was an unmarried mother with a baby daughter called Anna. In the past, Tina's mama had invited Kirsty to stay on the farm during her holidays from a large estate where she was in charge of a dairy herd. Thus Kirsty came to regard Tina's home as hers, since she had no family of her own.

She was still young, and strong as an ox. She did some of the heavy work, such as the weekly laundry. Cooking was on a large scale, what with farmhands (six of them in later years) sitting down for two hot meals a day.

The daily baking, cheese- and butter-making and looking after three young children was a hard task for a newly-widowed woman. Not forgetting the fact that at the time there was no electricity, and water had to be pumped from the well. It meant an awful lot of fetching and carrying to the farm animals as well, during the winter months when they were tethered or penned up.

With snow up to three to four metres deep and ice so thick on ponds and rivers, the farmers would take short-cuts, driving across with cars and tractors. Of course, in the summer it was easier, when the animals were out in the pasture and could drink their fill from any brook or a river inlet running through the farmland.

Luckily, Tina's mama was braver and more resourceful than you might expect. Over the years that followed, she became a self-taught vet, with a bag of syringes, penicillin, bandages and other items needed. In no time she was very much in demand by other farmers, to help a newborn calf, foal or piglets safely into this world. In return they offered free labour on the farm, so there was no money exchanged, since Tina's mama wasn't a registered vet.

Also through her visits, often nocturnal around the village, she became well known and liked. So much so that she ended up being a godmother to sixteen children. An honour, no doubt, but it meant a lot of birthday and Christmas presents. And not one was ever forgotten, till they reached the age of seventeen!

Soon, the income from the farm increased, from the sale

of milk, eggs and meat. Pigs, lambs and calves were sent to a slaughter-house. Whenever a van called for a livestock, Tina would run into the woods and cry her heart out, having fed and petted the calves and lambs since they were born. Some of them even had names, but sadly they had to be sold.

2

Tina was only ten years old when mama decided to build an upmarket dairy-house. One section was a pigsty and another was for poultry, with an intake of a thousand three-day-old chicks every year around Easter time. Half of them grew to be cockerels and were killed very young. So the family had gourmet feasts of tender *poussin*, done in cream and wild mushroom sauce for a long time to come. The main section of the building was for dairy cows, with automatic watercups built into the concrete structure. Above these were hatches so that the hay could be dropped into the trough from the loft above. The dairy kitchen had a large water tank, and another for cooling the milk churns. There was a woodburning stove with a huge iron pot for mixing the animal feeds with hot water. Molasses was added for the pig food, to fatten them up faster for market. It really was a large and complex brick and wood-frame building, painted red, with white-glossed window frames. Red tiles were used for roofing, thus paying lower insurance premiums. The timber was cut from the nearby woods and there were up to fifteen men on the building site, meaning that the work was finished in less than a year.

For the opening there was a barn dance; an open house for up to three hundred people, with a six-man band to keep everyone hopping. The farm now had electricity as well, with tall pylons dotting the farmyard and continuing in a straight line through the woodland to the neighbouring farms. A fridge, a freezer and an electric cooker soon appeared next to the woodburning stove.

Since Tina's mama toiled away all hours, from the age of seven Tina did her very best to lend a helping hand. She fed the animals, milked the cows, cooked and cleaned. After a four-kilometre trek from the village school it was a quick change into overalls and wellies, before any tea or homework. The farm thrived and expanded, and mama kept her war widow's pension a closely guarded secret, the only mention of it being a reason for not remarrying, although there was many a suitor who came calling!

The next venture was a sugar refinery, a cooperative started by the village farmers. For years botanists and scientists were under the impression that the climate in Finland was too cold to grow sugarbeet, but in fact it was a success. And as a bonus, the shareholders had all that sugar, syrup and molasses free from the factory! Thus Tina toiled away and became a real tomboy, made strong by competing with the farm labourers. Little Anna stayed for three months every summer, playing with the animals and having fun.

Tina's siblings didn't take much part in the dairy side of the farm. In fact, sister Irene would hold her nose when at close quarters to a cow! However, she enjoyed baking cakes and biscuits, and picking wild berries in the woods. Brother Leo was a born country squire, big and strong. Sadly, he didn't use that strength for work but preferred to sleep atop a haystack in the barn through busy summer days or entertain his cronies to a barbecue and the sauna!

Summers in Finland are beautiful and hot, but rather short. Most city-folk have a summerhouse by a lake and a speedboat to enjoy the elements. And there is so much to choose from, what with 60,000 lakes scattered around the country.

At the age of eight Tina had joined the Brownies and was able to partake of the above pleasures, camping out for a week annually. At the age of twelve she helped to care for Ada, an invalid lady who was paralysed from the waist down and lived in a specially-adapted bungalow. Her condition was due to a wilful act of throwing herself under an oncoming train, still in her wedding dress after being jilted at the altar. Many a farmer's wife called as was their duty and ran out in tears after a tongue lashing and missiles being thrown after them.

That's when Tina stepped in, to see how she fared. She rather enjoyed the encounters. She would call in with shopping, fetch water from the well and firewood from the shed. Often she had a welcome cup of tea and a slice of cake; at other times, she had to duck when a log was aimed at her head. All in all, Ada was a very independent lady, over seventy in years and still 'at war' with the groom who stood her up all those years ago!

These daily battles and cosy chats went on until Tina was sixteen and went off to attend a business college in the nearest town, some eighty kilometres away. She was to share a bedsit with sister Irene who had already finished her college education and was working as a cashier in a bank.

3

At the college Tina did very well in her studies, especially in mathematics, algebra, commercial law and foreign languages, taking Swedish and English. The choice was from five, including German, French and Russian.

The college was situated in the old part of the town, called Turku. It was close to the market square and surrounded by impressive town houses. In one of them dwelled a Swedish-speaking Jewish family with one son, Raymond. He was twenty-two and a reporter for both Finnish and Swedish television. And he was a proud owner of a very fast fibreglass speedboat. His father was an architect and his mother had exclusive boutiques selling leatherware, both in Turku and Stockholm.

Raymond's parents were on the board of governors at Tina's college. And so their son fell for her – a shy, seventeen-year-old country girl. It was all so proper then; a Barbara Cartland kind of old-fashioned courtship. One day a telegram arrived at the farm during the holidays: an invitation for tea at the Reither household. Tina felt very apprehensive, having never met the parents before, and was in for a shock. The maid brought in a heavy silver tea-service while the parents prepared Tina as to what she had to face. Their son had been having severe migraines for some time and the tests had proved that he had a brain tumour. The operation had been carried out at a private clinic in Stockholm three weeks earlier. But there remained a likelihood that the tumour had spread too far. When Tina was led to Raymond's bedside she realised that he was blind. His head was heavily bandaged and he was wearing tinted spectacles to minimise her shock. Tina was asked to spoonfeed him while catching up with all that had happened while she had been away in the country.

The following week Raymond was back at the hospital near to the college. Almost daily Tina was summoned to the headmaster's office to be informed that Mr Reither had rung; he would have to leave the hospital shortly, and would Tina take over? Showing some reluctance the headmaster told her quite firmly to skip so and so class and go to the hospital.

A few weeks went by, spoonfeeding and holding hands; and by then Tina was wearing an engagement ring. One morning, Mr Reither caught up with Tina on her way to college across the market square. He grabbed her by the shoulders and sobbed his grief: during the night his only son had passed away peacefully. Would Tina remember to visit his grave with roses from time to time?

After that she didn't have much contact with Raymond's parents until she was close to obtaining her diploma. They had been spending more time in Stockholm as they had close relatives there. Before leaving to spend at least a week on the farm Tina was invited to tea; and what a tea it was! She was confronted by a very unexpected proposition. The Reithers wanted to adopt her; to replace their son with a daughter; a good sort and still an innocent! She would have such riches and almost a jetset lifestyle! Tina's mind was reeling from the encounter with prominent citizens, but almost strangers.

What Tina didn't know at the time was: that 'daddy Reither' had done his homework to discover that Tina's grandfather was knighted and was Jewish. However, she took a firm stand; no amount of riches would sway her loyalties and cause her to desert her dear mama, Linda.

Prior to all this Tina's sister Irene was 'a pain in the neck'. She was in love; and as they had only one double bed, Tina was often ordered out into the dark streets when she should have been preparing for her final exams. On a few occasions there were three of them on that bed!

Irene would boast about Ari being in advertising and design! However, Tina took one look at his hands on the sly and knew that the fellow was telling 'porkies'. They were rough and red and the nails were broken; he was someone who did manual work rather than using his brain. This turned out to be true. One afternoon Tina saw him come through the gates of a cement factory! Mind you, he was good-looking; a real ladies' man; but apart from that, he was like a gun without bullets! In other words, useless; and a heavy drinker. Tina was trying to warn her sister that the man was trouble!

Irene resented it very much and became difficult to live with. She had already discovered the truth herself but they married hastily, as by then Irene was pregnant. It was a year later that Ari's drinking got out of hand and he was sent to a drying-out clinic for alcoholics for six months!

4

Long before going to college Tina's mama had told her about her grandfather's background. How this captain of a luxury ocean liner travelled regularly to the port of Turku. His wife accompanied him on most trips with a wicker basket for two pet tortoises as her babies as she couldn't have children. So, the captain took a fancy to Tina's grandmother, Alexandra, and they had two children from a six-year affair. Tina's auntie was named Bella Alexandra and her father William Leonard.

Captain Ashton had an eighteen-bedroomed mansion on the Devon coast in England. He acknowledged his children and for this reason Tina could never say that her father was a 'bastard'; oh, no, daddy was born 'out of wedlock'! As for auntie Bella, she had died of tuberculosis before Tina was born. Listening to this story an idea began to ferment in Tina's mind: to learn English, and go over there; as in following one's roots.

She was fortunate to get a job in a bank as a trainee accountant straight from college, getting glowing references from her headmaster. With all the trials and tribulations with Raymond and the Reithers, he had become almost a father-figure. Tina would never forget his parting words when she received her diploma: 'Whatever you do, do it well; for only the best is good enough!'

The impending adoption plans and Irene's problems soon came to a head. Irene's first son was christened Petri, and Tina was his god-mother. Irene was under a great deal of

10

pressure and soon something just snapped. When Tina proudly showed her her very first payslip from the bank, Irene removed her shoe and hit Tina on the head with such force that the stiletto heel drew a lot of blood and her payslip turned the colour of crimson! All because Tina was earning more than herself, although she had worked in another bank for over two years!

An incident like that can decide many things: to forgive and to forget or to get away – far away?

As there was no sisterly love, it was substituted by envy and hate.

5

So, Tina started saving like mad towards her airfare to England. Most girls in those days (this was 1961) came over as au pairs; but that wasn't to Tina's liking. She managed to wiggle all the relevant documents to come over as an exchange student via the Ministry of Agriculture. She was 'an old hand' in all that farming entails! And so she ended up on an estate in Worcestershire. A nice location and close to Malvern Winter Gardens where she could attend jazz concerts with her new-found friends. All were exchange students from various countries. Great; Tina had never encountered foreigners before! It was more like an adventure; to do a day's work in the fields or tend to dairy stock, attend evening classes, go to a disco, and her very first visit to a pub; to sample Babycham!

But perhaps it was too perfect to last. In such a tranquil setting there lurked a man with evil thoughts. He was none other than the son of the gentle, charming old gentleman owner of the estate.

On one summer's evening when Tina was checking and closing up the hen coops against hungry foxes, above a hillock appeared a man astride a black stallion! His aim was to take her there and then; tapping his crop on his shiny boot. But his arrogance soon turned to shame. Before he could remove any of Tina's clothing he was flat on his back and it was Tina holding the riding crop to send man and horse on their way!

There's a lot to be said for benefits of hard work to boost one's strength to take an opponent unawares!

No fuss was made of the incident. However, the secretary at the estate office suggested that Tina should move to her home, a nearby farm. Her mum could do with help in the kitchen and her father with potato-picking and the lambing season was yet to come. So Tina joined the Henderson family and was happy there until her exchange permit expired.

Soon after her move an official letter arrived from Finland reminding her of the consequences of breaking her contract and the likelihood of being recalled home unless she had an explanation and a good reason for moving. It was obvious that the man on the horse wasn't amused and had been busy writing.

Tina wrote too, in her defence, ending the letter with a heartfelt poem: 'Blonde, blue eyes; and charmed by the Northern Lights!'

The reply came that since it was obvious that Tina could take care of herself she could stay put! As for the owner of the estate and his wife, they invited Tina for cocktails on Christmas Eve. There was no mention of their son, but it was unspoken that they felt very sorry about it. Such a gesture from landed gentry goes a long way towards forgiveness and forgetting!

6

On her return home Tina settled in Helsinki, although her old job in the bank was open for two years for her to return to at any time. But Tina began to work for the Ministry of Defence at an army training centre on a private island, four kilometres from the city. There were around seven hundred men to only thirty women in catering, and other civilian personnel.

As some of the men were already married and didn't get any home leave for the first four months an order was issued to the female quarters to register for a judo course at the former Olympic Stadium in Helsinki. The man at the top regarded self-defence as paramount on an island where the male/female ratio was so unbalanced.

Tina gained a black belt after six months of throwing, grabbing and pulling every which way possible! A great time was had by all, especially at the officers' mess, where they could dance with fellows covered in epaulettes and medals.

The female block was a four-storey building with automatic light switches on the concrete staircase. One evening Tina returned from town late and was grabbed into an armlock from behind.

A corporal had been standing behind the main door in wait. In a flash Tina threw him on the floor and for a panicky moment feared that she had just killed the man because he just didn't move. There was nothing for it but to give her attacker the kiss of life!

It wasn't pleasant to say the least, as she was overcome by

14

his beer fumes! When she had revived the corporal he showed much remorse. In any case, he had got the wrong woman. He had been hoping for another. He was newly-married and had been able to postpone his compulsory army service to finish his university studies. Tina had no heart to spoil his career and decided not to report him. The man was so well-spoken and terrified of her. She believed that the lesson learned was more of a deterrent than any court martial or a prison term.

Such are man's needs that a beast in them takes over all reason in pursuit of their desire. Poor chap, he was a long way from his wife! And how he was going to explain the bump on his head and possible concussion was his affair!

7

During her weekend visits to the farm Tina would get together with her childhood friend Pirjo, who lived on a neighbouring farm. They had gone to school together and had cycled or skied there daily. During the long summer holidays they would visit in the evenings or go for a swim in the local river after sunset. They would swim across to the other side and compete against each other. On one of these outings Tina was ahead but in the middle of hitting a cold current she got a cramp on her leg and felt totally helpless and panicky. Thankfully, Pirjo wasn't far behind and saved her life by carrying her across in an armlock!

However, the experience was such that from then on Tina had a phobia about going into deep water. On venturing into sea she would swim along the shoreline, rather than out towards the horizon.

During the winter months the snow-covered landscape made a picture-postcard scene. The snow covered the ground in a soft blanket as white flour, and piled on tree branches and rooftops. When the weather was frosty the surface would be crispy and shimmer in the sunlight as crystals!

Tina loved skiing so much that every year, when there was enough snow on the ground, she would get her skis out and overdo her exercises. She had learned to ski almost as soon as she began to walk. Her first pair were no more than a metre long! In the course of her growing up they gradually became longer and she needed a new pair annually, as their

16

surface got scratched from wear and tear and they became too short.

The correct size was determined by standing the skis upright: you should be able to touch their tips with your fingertips. Even visitors and neighbours would use skis to go shopping or to visit for a gossip over afternoon coffee.

In later years Tina's skis were a designer set, and she had a similar outfit to go with them when she took part in competitions. She had to practise daily and during her college years often did so in the moonlight after finishing her homework.

Her training circuit was marked by red ribbon tied to trees, so that she wouldn't get lost in the limited light.

The competitions were thirty or forty kilometres of cross-country treks. Every ten kilometres a steward would give the competitors a glass of hot milk to avoid dehydration. At the finishing line Tina was so 'jiggered' that she was unable to undo the catches in her skis and was practically carried off to the sauna. But the main thing was that she usually won, although pushed to the very limits of her endurance. Over such a long distance there was a lot of uphill climbing, but it was sheer ecstasy to zoom down the slopes at speeds of up to ninety miles an hour!

When Tina had been an inter-counties champion for two years she faced a lot of dirty tricks and sabotage by the rival teams. One of the more dangerous tricks was putting coarse salt on an icy track on a fast downhill slope. It would melt the ice into a soggy patch and your skis would get stuck or slow your speed if not cause a nasty fall.

Tina was prepared, and carried a piece of wax candle in her inside pocket, not easy to detect. She used this to rub off the salty snow and try to make up for lost time. Occasionally, there was a faller at a bottom of a hill; as you couldn't run over someone it meant a quick diversion between the trees, with a limited space to manoeuvre at high speed.

17

There were times when Tina found herself flat on her back on a snow-mound and her skis, lovely red and yellow in design in smithereens all around her! She had been very fortunate never to hurt herself or break any bones, as had happened to some of the others taking part.

Tina couldn't think of any other sport that was so rewarding or exhilarating. It put you in touch with nature's elements; the pure scenery and clear air made you quite lightheaded!

That winter, when she was working in the bank, she started off on the first snow of the year around mid-morning when her flatmates were still having a snooze. It felt so good that she lost all her bearings as there were not yet any marked trails.

She recalled crossing a few railway lines, but didn't see any road signs. As a result, by dusk she found herself on the outskirts of Helsinki! She had started off in Turku and would have travelled over a hundred miles without stopping.

The only way back was to catch a train. Her flatmates were worried sick by the time she returned around ten p.m. She hadn't needed any food; only handfulls of snow for her thirst.

On Sunday morning she was so stiff that her flatmates had to lift her out of bed to go to the loo! Various exercises all day long and hot soaks in the tub got her going enough to be able to turn up for work at the bank by Monday morning.

But she soon began to miss her friends and the English way of life, and made a firm decision to return.

8

The Trust House Forte hotel group advertised in a national newspaper: 'Jobs for Finnish girls, papers and permits arranged and no experience required'. So, in 1963, Tina returned, and to what a welcome! She was grateful to Sir Charles Forte for leading the way in being staff-oriented. A young secretary was at the railway station with a black limousine to welcome her and drive her to a hotel located in Moreton-in-the-Marsh, a cosy little country hamlet.

Later on Tina asked for a transfer to The Queens Hotel, located on the seafront in Hastings. By then it was summer and it made good sense to combine swimming and sunbathing with waitressing!

Towards the end of the season, one Sunday afternoon a shadow fell over her while sunbathing on the beach. A total stranger, Mr Minsk, said, 'You are too young to be here, the rest of the folk in Hastings are retired!'

'What are you going to do about it?'

'Well, I have six restaurants in London. Why don't you come to take a look? See which you like best, and come and work for me?'

Tina ventured to ask, 'Obviously, you are not retired, so why are you in Hastings?'

'I also own that bingo hall over there, and come over on weekends to check up on takings. So, what do you say?'

'Not a lot just now, but I will speak to my friend Romano. He is an Italian waiter at my hotel.'

'I know him quite well. If you think that I am trying to pick you up, Romano could come with you to visit my restaurants in London.'

And so it was arranged. Tina chose to work at The Four Seasons restaurant in Bond Street. As the third Sunday arrived and Tina was all packed she called to ask Mr Minsk: 'Since you want me so bad, come and get me!'

He did too, with a very snazzy sports car. Thus Tina learned the meaning of 'headhunting'.

He drove to a garage near a block of flats in St John's Wood, where he had a smart bachelor pad. Tina was to stay overnight and sleep on a sofa. In the morning he would take her to Willesden Green where he had a spare room going.

He prepared a light breakfast of grapefruit, toast and coffee, asking Tina to roll up her bedding and take it to the car. At his property in Willesden, on the ground floor there was a small cafeteria and above his offices. The company was registered as Aaron Holdings Ltd. There was a bedroom with a bathroom en-suite, where the chef had stayed before Tina's coming.

On arrival Ivo Minsk had second thoughts: 'You have to come and go through the café, and I have a safe in there. Can I trust you?'

'Well, if your money goes walkabout then you'll know who to blame, since I am the only one living here. Should there be a break-in then you have to find the culprit outside!'

Tina enjoyed her work at The Four Seasons, although the hours were very long: from twelve noon to midnight. Most nights Ivo turned up to drive her home, always pretending to make sure that she locked the place up properly! But she suspected that his real reason was to check that she didn't take any boyfriends to her room in Willesden.

About Ivo: he was a hard-nosed businessman, but a true gent. He was fighting a temptation to get familiar but he never crossed that line. Of course he was thirty years Tina's senior.

All was well for some time, but there was a catch, as in so many situations there is. Tina's work permit was for resident/catering, which meant that she had to live in the same premises where she worked. Since Willesden Green is some distance from Bond Street it couldn't continue. As a foreign national of alien status, every time that Tina moved she had to report her new address at a local police station. So, she parted company with Ivo Minsk amicably.

Taking this walk along memory lane thirty years back is a long trek; here is hoping that all of you readers are still following Tina's footsteps. It might stir your own memories of the good old Sixties?

9

Next, Tina settled in at an exclusive, privately-owned hotel in Harrington Gardens, Kensington. A large proportion of the clientele were Japanese businessmen and tourists. Also, sports personalities, especially cricketers, were much in evidence. And, according to a barman, one resident was a high-class tart who was very partial to cricketers!

'To be sure, it takes all sorts!' was Tina's comment.

The general manager was very fussy about presentation and detail. Most of the staff, especially the chambermaids, were German, and the chef was a Scotsman. He and the manager hated each other and had many a heated argument for all to hear.

Sam Lightman enjoyed a fillet of steak and often had it for lunch. He had made it known that he didn't want any trimmings. There was a new German girl, called Ulrika, whom Tina was training in waitressing and silver service. One day, at the close of the lunch hour, when the last of the customers were leaving the dining-room, Ulrika very properly served Mr Lightman's steak with a side salad, saying: 'Sir, you must eat the watercress, because it is good for a cock!'

Tina thought: 'Oh, dear God, no; the Scot had done it again!'

Sam Lightman got up like a shot, heading for the kitchen, knowing that the chef had asked Ulrika repeat that parrot fashion, and sacked him on the spot!

Meanwhile, Ulrika ran to Tina saying: 'I must have done something wrong; now I must go?'

'No, nothing of the sort; it's the chef who is going!'

So, Tina explained to her, that she must never say a word which she doesn't know the meaning of; and keep going to evening classes, to improve her English. Tina herself didn't know whether watercress was an aphrodisiac, so she made out that the gist of it was: after eating his steak, smothered in watercress, Mr Lightman was expected to hop into bed with a woman and do Romeo and Juliet!

In due course, Ulrika became a first-class waitress, but very economical with conversation with customers; only what was necessary!

As for the chef, nothing but negative could be said about his personality, although his culinary skills were above average and the basis of his getting the job in the first place.

The head waiter lived in Brighton. His name was Terry, and he was a lovely man to work with. One evening, before catching his train, he asked Tina and the head porter, John, to join him for a drink at a local pub in Gloucester Road. There was no seating available so the three of them stood in the centre of the floor. Terry was sipping from his pint with great contentment until his wrist went limp and his pint was upside down!

Everyone was in fits of laughter, and taking bets about it ever happening again. Poor Terry was so tired, in fact he was dead beat, after all it had been an exceptionally busy day, in the cause of which he had already changed his shirt, to perk him up!

It was decided that if a man was too tired to hold onto his pint the best thing for it is to go home!

While working there Tina discovered two great dance venues. First The Empire Ballroom in Leicester Square, and later the Café de Paris in Piccadilly. Both venues had two resident bands. At The Empire, Joe Loss and his orchestra and Ken McIntosh and his big band; both with two vocalists who were vying for the limelight! Tina and her generation were so fortunate to dance to music that was the real thing; none of today's DJs playing canned or taped tunes! And there were boyfriends galore; she had a few on the go at any given time. When some of them became too persistent Tina took off for the country, for peace and quiet.

10

Tina went to a small hotel near St Albans which had a very highly rated restaurant, frequented by filmcrews, actors and singing groups from Elstree Studios. She saw the Beverly Sisters when they were young and riding high.

From St Albans she travelled to London every week to spend her one day off work. She had a Finnish girlfriend, who worked at The Carrick Hotel in Leicester Square, and would 'smuggle' Tina in to share her single bed. Her trips followed very much the same pattern: in the afternoon she would see a film; Doris Day and Rock Hudson together was a pleasure to watch. The other pinups of the time were Tony Curtis, Jack Lemmon, Clark Gable, Clint Eastwood, Remi Sneider, Sophia Loren, Vivian Leigh, Audrey Hepburn, Grace Kelly and Julie Andrews. After the cinema they would have dinner and head for Café de Paris. Once in a while, Tina hit it lucky and got a lift home all the way to Hertfordshire. In the autumn and winter she had to remind any driver who hadn't ventured onto that road before to watch out for fog-pockets which were notorious on lower ground. And at the end of the journey, what did they get? Nothing! Just a quick kiss as there was a nightporter and a black Labrador called Jet, waiting. Needless to say, not one man came twice!

There wasn't much to do in the evenings, as the hotel was four miles from St Albans. So, to pass the time, Tina took up dressmaking for herself and knitted jumpers, socks and mittens for her nephews in Finland.

Apart from keeping any boyfriends at arm's length or

simply not finding 'the right one', Tina had long walks with Jet. How clever he was! As soon as Tina settled in her room in the staff section, which was on the second floor, there was Jet, scratching outside the door wanting to go 'walkies'. Still, it was very pleasant recreation for both of them, exploring various country lanes and recalling similar walks back home a long way away. After a year of quiet life, Tina became restless, which was inevitable, and went back to London. Her next job was at a private members' club off Oxford Street. Most of the older members had been in the colonial services and military in the Far East. The new members were their sons or friends, recommended for membership. These were eminent Harley Street physicians, directors of commerce, culture and the arts, and aristocrats. The cream of society: collectively they had a finger in every pie!

Tina was often asked why she came over to England, when living standards in Finland were so high. Her stock replay was to say: 'To improve my English and follow my grandfather's roots.' On only one occasion did she expand on her reasons. She was serving a dinner table for six men, two of whom were club members and the other four their guests, whom Tina had never seen before. Once again she was asked why she came over to England. When Tina mentioned that her grandfather hailed from Devon, one of them asked his name, and which part of the Devon coast he lived. Tina answered: 'From Paignton, and the name of the gentleman is the later Sir Alex Ashton.' Getting bold, she added that, 'One of these days I shall look it up and claim my rightful legacy.'

No more was said on the subject, as Tina was too busy clearing the dishes from their table to observe their faces for any reaction of shock or panic.

She was paid to do a job and did a full day's work. She was at the club a total of three and a half years, and for the last year she was paid a retainer so that the club could save face in connection with the events yet to unfold. She was asked to stay until her work permit expired and the decision was reached at a full board meeting. It was 1968, and Tina was now free from the work permit restrictions; she could take up any occupation, start a business and even apply for British citizenship. She hadn't planned on any inquiries until such a time, but the tide turned against her, before she got started. Nor did she receive the usual welcome as when she started working in the club. Half the staff were so old that they should have retired years ago, or so they seemed to a young newcomer.

Tina overheard two old maids in their seventies talking in the stillroom where they both worked. Amy was saying to Alice: 'What you make of that blonde? Should have gone to Hollywood, rather than come here.' The answer from Alice was: 'With a figure like that and cocky as anything, mark my words, she'll never stick to waitressing.'

True, Tina had what was called 'A French figure', her vital statistics being 40-26-36. She was five feet eight inches tall and her legs were long; they just ran and ran and were lithe and strong from all that skiing. However, she had no acting talent, nor aspirations for a glamorous life. Except for expensive clothes. At the Café de Paris she had met an older man, Max, who was in the rag trade and also a Freemason. A friend of his had a shop near Carnaby Street. Max took her over there quite often to try on designer dresses that had been worn just once in fashion shows in Europe: Milan, Paris and Amsterdam. They were so elegant and Tina got them for a fraction of the true price. And she was very particular about her shoes; they had to match her handbag, outfit and hair colour. This started at an early age. Her godmother was a village hairdresser, so Tina had a free cut on her golden tresses.

The club secretary, Mr Allan, was 'a sweetiepie' and the general manager, Mr Ball, was okay too, but often bad-tempered; either from a hangover or gasping for the next pint! The two head waiters, Mr Haines, who was Welsh, and Mr Hans, who was German, were easy to get on with. The rest of the staff were a mixed bag, except for one who stood out and was called Stella. She was to become Tina's long-term friend and ally. She had 'crossed the water' from Ireland two years earlier, leaving her nursing career to work in catering. The rest of her family were left behind in County Cork, except for her sisters, Paula and Mary, who were both well established in London, long before Stella joined them. Stella's parents often invited Tina to spend holidays with them. Unfortunately she never got around to going, as she went to Finland every summer for three weeks to give her dear mama a break.

At the club there was one cheeky porter called Jimmy. He was always saying, 'The grass in Ireland is so green, the likes of it you can't find anywhere in the world!'

Tina was intrigued, having seen grass aplenty, paler and darker shades, so she had to ask: 'What is the secret of its colour?'

Jimmy was grinning from ear to ear: 'Why, because nobody ever walks on it, they're all over here!'

Once he was having a heated discussion with another porter, called Jack, about the other's girlfriend not being much to look at. Jack got one over him by replying: 'Look, mate, you don't look at the mantelpiece when poking the fire!'

The porters were very keen on betting on the horses as there was a telex behind the porters' lodge which received the results from meetings at the end of each race. Tina was pulled into their activities and she learned to study form and weights, and got so interested that she opened an account at the nearest bookie, and made telephone bets. After all, it wasn't very ladylike to walk into a betting shop and half the time she was too busy working. She had beginner's luck and won every time for the first month. The minimum bet by phone was £5.00; don't forget that this was in 1967. But all good things must come to an end, and she started losing. After a week of that she was prudent enough to come to a full stop and keep her savings in the bank.

The club was residential, and therefore the catering staff served three meals a day. Breakfast started at seven-thirty and dinner finished at nine-thirty. Of course there was a break between the meals. There was also a number of private functions to cater for, such as weddings, coming-of-age parties and graduation celebrations for sons and daughters of club members. Most had a country residence and only stayed at the club during the week. Most were men, but there was a ladies' room for lunch for members and their guests. For breakfast and dinner, wives and female relatives would join the men in the main dining room.

Tina and Stella lived life to the full. Apart from work they went everywhere together, shopping for new outfits every few weeks. Both had standing appointments at the same hairdressers twice a week. They would sunbathe in Grosvenor Square or Hyde Park, and took afternoon tea at The India Tea Centre in Oxford Street. Sometimes they would go to hear the music at The Café de Paris at the afternoon tea dance for a couple of hours. Back at the club they would quickly change into their green uniforms, with white cuffs and collars, serve dinner, bathe, change again into something sexy, hop into a taxi and by ten-thirty they were back on the dance floor at 'The Caf'. It was all running by a tight schedule; oh, what energy you have, when young! None of today's drugs were in evidence; the joy of living was more than enough!

Not forgetting the house parties on Saturday nights. Tina was always invited, whether it was in a bedsit in Turnpike Lane or Finsbury Park, or in a posh house in Knightsbridge or Richmond. However, Stella dropped out of these capers, as she wanted to put some time aside to visit her sisters.

And all those fellows at The Café de Paris! There was so much choice. The regulars, who got nicknamed as 'Allbran', the young and the over fifties, visiting businessmen from America, Australia, Canada, Europe, Scandinavia and the Eastern Bloc, and even a few who sneaked in from the House of Commons, with their briefcases and brollies. Just as well that there was a secure cloakroom to leave their secret documents!

And all that dancing! Tina loved the tango, waltz and rumba. What is it they say about MPs; having their snout in every trough!?

When later on long evening dresses became the fashion the ladies made an elegant gathering. So no wonder some MPs wanted to take a look in and keep on coming! To hold on to a government minister gave a whole new meaning to a tango; rather than partnering any Tom, Dick or Harry, not forgetting 'Allbran'. After all, Princess Margaret held her eighteenth birthday party there, and Elizabeth Taylor took to the floor on her visits to London.

In two years of partying, Tina had a few proposals, but wanted to stay fancy-free and footloose a while longer, as she was only twenty-three at the time. The money went such a long way then, it was always a taxi, not a bus or the Tube, and there were foreign holidays every summer. Tina had free bed and board at the club, and generous bonuses twice annually, as tipping was not allowed. The club actually closed for three weeks every summer, for any major cleaning or redecoration. The other gentlemen's clubs offered hospitality to resident members, and the staff all had their holidays at the same time.

11

At the beginning of 1968 Tina finally met 'the right man', who was called Fabian, and they got engaged that same year. Fabian hailed from Trinidad, and was of mixed parentage. His mother was Indian and his father French. He was already 32, and had been a police inspector, but had always wanted to practise law. He was a student at The Middle Temple for three years, before qualifying with first-class honours. He was also the vice-president of the student union and Tina was able to attend their parties and group debates. They were planning to emigrate to Canada; Fabian as a lawyer and Tina as his legal secretary. Thus she decided to do an Open University degree in business and commercial law. She bought some of her own books but also made good use of Fabian's. He was short of funds, being a full-time student, so Tina offered to pay his rent for a bedsit in Tooting Bec. She also bought him a second-hand car with the money saved from her brief gambling venture. She stayed with him over the weekends. Fabian would pick her up on Friday and return her to the club Monday morning on his way to college. In his final year he was unwilling to accept any more financial help and got a part-time position working for the Board of Trade in the City. He was a good sort, and often popped into a church for meditation, instead of making a beeline to the nearest pub. During their long engagement they became very close; Fabian would even cut Tina's toenails, and loved brushing her hair, referring to it as 'golden thread'. So many young couples lived together, even when they had only just met, but not Tina, although in the last two years she could have done so, being now self-employed, managing tenement properties in Kensington and Knightsbridge.

In Finland, the laws were very strict; at the time it was an offence for unmarried couples to cohabit. A lone female couldn't even have a male lodger, lest they 'got up to no good'! In this aspect Tina followed the Finnish way. In any case it was more fun to visit each other for some nocturnal activities. As for Café de Paris, no more flirting; Tina and Fabian would only go Saturday night once a week.

Tina exchanged letters with her mama, keeping her up to date with all her doings. Lately she had been complaining about arthritis in her shoulder, news that Tina shared with Fabian. Soon it was time for her annual summer holidays; Fabian escorted her to the ship, carrying a box, his present to Tina's mum. It was an electric mixer, to make all that whisking and blending so much easier on her poorly arm. At the club many members and all the staff knew where Tina spent her holidays and that she travelled by sea. That particular ship was named *Michael Khalinin*, which travelled via Le Havre, Harwich, Copenhagen, Malmo and Helsinki to Leningrad. Tina's cabin mate was an Estonian lady in her fifties. She had been trying for a number of years to obtain a visa and had finally succeeded in getting one. Now she was on her way to visit her sister. Marion was a matron in a hospital in Manchester, and her husband was a surgeon on the same unit.

They had been married for 25 years, but had no children. She was a lovely person to meet, and Fabian felt the same, although their meeting was rather brief, as visitors were ordered to leave the ship shortly. On the three-night crossing and the stopovers, Marion and Tina compared notes about working and living in a foreign country, and their contact with family and friends back home. On board the ship there was caviar for breakfast and lots of other goodies. There was also a dance band that pulled Tina like a magnet. Marion came along to watch for a while, until one of the uniformed chaps claimed Tina as his partner for the evening. he was a first officer called Victor. On the second night more of the same followed until the early hours. Victor was trying to entice Tina to his cabin for a nightcap, but as she was engaged she had no intention of going. On their last evening, Tina decided to try her hand in a poker game with a group of African students on their way to Leningrad to study at the university there. Victor didn't seem to approve. Marion and Tina decided to have an early night and retired to their bunks before eleven. Without even knocking on the door, in walked Victor. Tina made it known that his behaviour was diabolical! But unconcerned he sat on the side of her bunk saying that he was only a messenger. Tina was invited to the captain's cabin for a farewell party. It became obvious that he wouldn't budge without Tina going along. She was concerned for Marion's privacy, and got dressed. She put on her black cocktail dress with low cleavage and her high-heeled shoes. Only, when they got there did she realise that there was no party and that she was the only guest! Heavy mahogany double doors closed behind them. Victor stood by them throughout. Around an oval table sat six men, five of them in dress uniform, but not in the colours of the navy. One of them was dressed in civilian clothes and acted as a spokesman. Tina had to collect her wits to calm her nerves to cope with such an unexpected turn of events. Each of the men introduced themselves, stating their rank. All of which went over her head, 'like water off a duck's back'.

Was it due to panic or more likely the realisation of what they represented. The 'main host' made a great fuss, pulling a chair out for her, saying that the very same chair was sat in by John F. Kennedy on his recent state visit!

His next statement followed: 'You are an ideal lady for us; competent in self-defence, used to dealing with military personnel and trustworthy, since you have sworn an oath of confidentiality twice.' Tina's mind went into an overdrive, realising that this band of men knew about her judo training and working in a bank and army headquarters in Helsinki. she agreed that these were the facts. There wasn't a lot she could have said, but for some reason she became interested as to what they were leading up to. The leader of the pack then asked her to work for them as a KGB informer. Not to disembark in Helsinki, but to travel with them to Leningrad. he offered her an annual retainer of £10,000 sterling, plus travel expenses. According to him, Tina was in an ideal position to gather and pass information about certain members of the club, as to whom they entertained and what they discussed. As a waitress she had an opportunity to get a gist of conversations. However, no names of any individuals were given. By this time, Tina's hackles were up; without further thought she said: 'Gentlemen, you have done your homework, but overlooked something very close to my heart. Are you not aware that my father was blown to bits by your army on the border. Furthermore, when the first Russian cars came out of your factories a neighbour bought one of them, and of course it was red. he proudly offered my dear mama a lift to a polling station. Do you know what her answer was? "No, thank you!" And what did she do? She ordered a minicab, requesting a Mercedes, and it had to be blue! That surely was a statement against communism. In fact it was a talk of the village for years to come. For the record, my political views have taken a similar stance.'

The spokesman's face went scarlet, the others were shifting about and the atmosphere became very tense. Tina then asked for something for her sudden headache. Victor produced two white tablets from his pocket, which she held in her palm. There was no sign of any bottles nor glasses (some party), so she asked him to get her a glass of water to wash them down.

Thus she plotted her escape from there. As soon as the doors opened, Tina got up in a flash, pushed Victor out of the way and ran like hell to Marion and safety. In the cabin, she wasn't sleeping, but sitting on tenterhooks saying, 'I was so worried for you, you don't know what they are capable of!'

'Who is?' Tina asked.

'The KGB, who else? After all, I grew up under their oppression!' Marion replied.

Tina then opened her fist to show Marion the tablets, asking: 'What are these?'

Marion studied them, saying, 'Don't take them unless you want to sleep all the way to Leningrad!'

According to her knowledge as a hospital matron they were a strong form of narcotic.

On disembarking, Marion stuck close to Tina like glue. They were to travel back in three weeks on another ship, and their cabin numbers corresponded.

12

On her arrival home Tina was in two minds; whether to tell her mama, or not? Would it upset her too much? Her other reasoning was, what if some strange men appeared at the farm to ask questions; as had happened after her previous visit? However, those men were genuine, from the DOE.

That summer Tina's mama was complaining about the state of roads and how bad it had been during the spring thaw. Tractors and lorries were getting stuck in the ruts of mud and water, as there was never any proper drainage and no solid foundations to the structure. The new settlers were high and dry, driving on their newly-constructed roads to their new homesteads!

Tina went to visit some neighbours on foot to take a closer look at the road in question. Being summer, it was dry, but she observed how the expansion of the ground had even exposed some tree roots and dislodged rather large stones.

So, on her return to London Tina had a plan under her hat! She had a good friend, Tarja, who worked at the Finnish embassy in Belgravia. Over the years they had visited the Finnish Church & Seamens' Club in Rotherhithe for coffee meetings and to unwind in the proper Finnish sauna. Every year before Christmas, members of the social club were invited to a bazaar and the Finnish ambassador and his wife were there to welcome the guests. On sale were homemade tree decorations made from straw, books, cookies and, best of all, reindeer meat!

For old times' sake Tina asked Tarja a favour: to get her

statistics and figures from the war office and the DOE as to what sort of grants were handed out to the new settlers to build their homes and especially what funding was allocated for their road construction?

Tarja was as good as gold, and passed on the relevant information, upon which Tina acted without further ado. She composed a very stern letter to the department of the environment, quoting the monies paid to evacuees, and compared that to her mama's situation. A woman alone running a farm, with the road leading to it in a sorry state or unpassable. She, if anyone, deserved a government grant to have it rebuilt, drainage and tarmac laid, and even straightened, as most of it ran through their own woodland. The way that a certain war widow had been overlooked simply wasn't cricket!

She didn't receive a reply, nor mentioned her actions to her mama so as not to give her any false hope. But the 'whizkids' of the mentioned government department acted with great speed. Thus mama had two unexpected visitors, with their aerial maps and plans to establish the borders of the farm. When mama asked what it was all about they mentioned that her daughter from London had given them a good telling off, adding, 'Quite a girl she must be too!'

The road was inspected and measured and in no time at all a substantial grant was awarded, so mama had the best road in the village.

Tina was very close to her mama, not only because of their bloodline but for all those years they had toiled away side by side like workmates in the summer evenings, often until midnight, weeding, spraying for insects and watering; even the mosquitoes had retired for the night long before the pair of them!

13

About the evacuees that Tina had referred to. She was already at primary school, which in Finland started at the age of seven, when they arrived from the Russian border, south-east of Finland. This is documented as 'a war settlement'. The Russian Republic confiscated a large parcel of land for it. Not only that, but for years to come after the war ended the famous Finnish shipbuilding yards were busy adding to the Russian fleet. The section of land to be relinquished was prime farmland. The families that had to uproot came in convoys across the country to settle on the south-west border.

They were a sorry sight; each brought a horse, pulling an antiquated cart, piled high with children, grandparents and their worldly goods, and one or more cows were tied by a rope to follow behind. But even they were different to any cow Tina had ever seen; they were the colour of red squirrels, not brown.

It was an order from the government that instructed farmers to give up a specified amount of land to the settlers and put them up in their homes. One room or more was to be allocated with use of the kitchen. And a warm welcome was expected, although not by the established order!

The farmers were compensated for their loss and inconvenience, while the evacuees built their homesteads nearby. As the folk in Tina's home county were Christian and prosperous farmers, human compassion prevailed. After all, the travellers were so inoffensive, grateful and doing their utmost to blend in. But their customs, and especially their dialect, were hard to understand, and half the time Tina was guessing.

Now she was contemplating ways to take mama's mind off what Tina had experienced. Although she didn't let on, but was busy with her new mixer, cooking, baking and entertaining. Most of the neighbours were in the habit of popping over for news from abroad and to see Tina. Since her mama had never been abroad, Tina decided that now was the time to start. In fact she insisted that a fortnight's break would be a treat for her, as she was quite capable and willing to 'run the show'; do the milking, feeding, baking and cooking.

So, mama contacted five of her women friends and off to Sweden they sailed! On her return she told of all that she had seen; Tina laughed so much that at the end of her report she was quite incoherent.

One that stands in memory is: mama seeing for the first time a black man, sitting in the sun, the question being as to what for? He couldn't possibly get a lighter shade of brown, when he was born black. Mama had a terrific sense of humour, which Tina had inherited, and it saved many a tricky situation when in a management position and dealing with staff. When it was time for Tina to return to London, Kirsty arrived to spend her annual holidays at the farm. She was alone, and had aged so much from all the sorrow of losing Anna, who had met a terrible end when she was only nineteen.

She had grown to be an extremely pretty girl, graceful like a newborn colt! However, her life had been a sad one, moving about from one farm to another, living in inadequate accommodation, tied to Kirsty's job.

Tina remembered many occasions when she would collect Anna from the farm before the start of the new school term. She would kick and scream, being pulled by her hair or getting a stick. Anna never wanted to leave, and before the time came to go she was so distressed that she would wet her bed. As a result, she didn't do well at school and on leaving went to work as a machinist at a factory, making bras and corsets.

When Tina worked in the bank she lived in a flatshare with friends she had made at college. One day, on returning from work, there sat Anna on her doorstep. She looked so unkempt and dirty, and her long hair was matted and tangled.

Tina didn't ask too many questions, as her appearance said it all. Inside the apartment, Tina suggested that a long soak in the bathtub would revive her spirits, but she no longer seemed to care. Tina had to manhandle her, strip her and wash her hair. After that, she got dressed in Tina's clothes, a bit on the large side but at least clean.

Tina showed her kindness, and gave her a good dinner and a warm bed. When Anna had fallen asleep, Tina rang her mama: 'Do you know why Anna seems to be destitute?'

It turned out that four days earlier she had arrived at the farm unexpectedly, subdued, and only stayed the night. When the morning came, mama and brother Leo found her gone. She had taken a bicycle, some banknotes from the bureau, and torn a page from mama's diary to get Tina's address in Turku.

Mama was hurt to see Anna 'gone bad' in resorting to theft, which was almost unheard of in the village. Such was the trust between neighbours and visitors that the front door was never locked during the day, only at night.

On learning this Tina didn't reprimand Anna for what she had done; after all they were about the same age at eighteen. But she couldn't trust her now to stay in the apartment when Tina and her flatmates went to work. After breakfast, Tina gave her all the cash that she had and advised Anna to go home to her mum.

And yet, she knew that wasn't going to happen. Through

40

all her hardships and beatings the bond had been severed. Looking back, it's almost as if she had come to say her final goodbyes to those who had shown her any kindness during her growing up years. Later, Tina was to learn that Anna had gone hitch-hiking, and Tina never saw her again, as it all ended a year later in Norway.

Her body was found in some woods, which were used for NATO exercises and training. She had been gang-raped and strangled. Tina cried buckets on learning this, by which time she was living in England. The case was heartbreaking. Her life had been one of misery and unsettled, like a leaf blown by the wind, except for those summer days with Tina's family, before it ended in tragedy.

14

On their return journey once again Tina and Marion were comparing notes, but this time it was about time spent with their loved ones. Throughout the trip the sea was stormy, and most passengers were seasick. There was no dancing, as even the cutlery and crockery were jumping about. On reaching terra firma, neither were aware that before boarding the outwardbound ship there had been activity behind the scenes. Their cabin had been bugged!

During the first week back at the club, Tina had some strange visitors. While in her room in the staff quarters, just back from the hairdressers, there was a knock at the door. The club secretary, Mr Allen, escorted them in. They introduced themselves as MI5 agents, asking if Tina's name was so and so? When she answered in the affirmative, one of them pronounced, 'You are a suspected enemy agent!'

Tina was flabbergasted, although she told them about the KGB's audacity to ask her to be their informer. They were particularly keen to know the extent of her friendship with Victor. Did she go to bed with him?

Tina pointed out that surely that was a lapse in their manners, when matters concerning state security appeared to be the main issue. He then added: 'As you are an alien, there is a likelihood you will be deported back home!'

All of a sudden, it flashed through her mind that that was exactly what the villain who had claimed fraudulent title to Tina's legacy in Devon had hoped to achieve. Get her out of the country, in a most foul manner, before she looked into the matter and started court proceedings. Although she had limited legal documents, as the solicitor's offices dealing with the will and deeds to the property of the late Sir Ashton had been burned down during the war. Or was it arson? There lay another mystery.

At the time of his death, his wife had passed on, and both Auntie Bella and father William were dead; the legacy was to pass on to their issue. Tina was a little one at the time and didn't remember meeting him, but according to mama she was the apple of his eye.

Thus mama decided, when Tina first travelled to England, to have a heart to heart with her, showing an enlarged photograph of a white, three-storey building, with columns and balconies. At the back of it were reference numbers and letters to legal documents, held in the solicitor's offices.

There was a phone-call for Tina on the switchboard, which she was to take in the secretary's office. Of all people it was Victor, the first officer from the ship.

He sounded very affable, as if nothing untoward had taken place. he was asking Tina for a date, and to meet him outside The Dominion in Tottenham Court Road, seven-thirty p.m. the following day, which was Thursday.

Tina told him straight out that she had no intention of going, that had he forgotten that she was engaged and very much 'a one man girl'. However, he was so persistent, and as Tina should have been getting back to work, just to get him off the line she promised to meet him at the appointed time and place. The following Monday, the same two men from MI5 paid her a second visit asking: 'Why didn't you go?'

Such a bold question indicated that there had been a tap on that phone conversation between herself and Victor.

Tina answered: 'Of course I didn't go, I am not that foolish!'

One of the men then divulged that they had waited for her to turn up for half an hour.

When Tina asked who was waiting for her, he answered: 'Us two and two from the other side; Victor brought a mate along!'

Tina laughed. 'Talk about fools, four grown men watching each other all that time!'

What the outcome of the evening would have been had Tina kept that date, it doesn't bear thinking about.

15

And so began a long saga of surveillance. The big-wigs of the KGB were trying to get back at Tina, since she had ruffled their feathers. Their stars and decorations didn't mean a thing!

At the same time, MI5 were busily vetting Tina's friends and contacts. She was bugged, watched and followed.

Before the week was over, Stella had some strange news.

Her sister Paula was in business with Boris, who was also her common-law husband. Two chaps from MI5 had paid them a visit one evening, questioning Boris. Asking about his political views and about his legal status as a resident in this country. They had divulged their knowledge about his past, when he was at a university in Krakow in Poland. He was known to have been a dissident, taking an active part in demonstrations and protests.

Boris had pointed out that it was all true, but these days he was too busy running a restaurant to even think about politics. So, they had left. But a few days later they had another visitor all the way from Poland: seventeen-year-old Kalinka, come to see her dad!

It was soon established that Boris's wife was very much alive and kicking. Paula, being Irish, expected Satan himself next through the door!

These events got her to such an extent that she sat in her car by Battersea Bridge all night, trying to decide whether to jump in or attach a hose to the exhaust pipe. But when the dawn broke and the sun rose over the Thames, Paula realised that she had a business to run and Boris was okay really; it was just that he forgot to mention a few things, such as having a wife and daughter!

Next came a long letter from Marion in Manchester. It was a sad tale, and so unfair for such a nice person.

On her return home, she found her husband and his car gone. He too had encountered unexpected visitors. It had been made clear to him that he had a choice; to leave the country or be charged with committing bigamy! Poor Marion found herself alone and single, after twenty-five years of happy marriage. And the hospital lost a brilliant surgeon, as he had returned to Estonia. Whether he rekindled his affections with his first and legal wife, Marion had no heart to find out.

Tina and Marion exchanged letters for years to come. She even visited her in London, when they would lunch together at The Four Seasons in Bond Street. But when Tina got married, they lost touch.

Fabian didn't escape either. On numerous occasions he found leaflets about communism, with Chairman Mao's picture emblazoned on the cover. These were left on his doorstep or pushed through the letterbox late into the night. As they went straight into a bin, another caper took more distasteful form. While working and studying in the city, men, strangers to him, approached, making homo-sexual advances.

On one occasion, when in a restaurant having his lunch, a city gent sat next to him and proceeded to squeeze his knee!

Fabian wasn't easily rattled, but this really got to him. When he came to pick Tina up that Friday evening, he looked like a thundercloud. He was so embarrassed about the whole thing, wanting to keep it to himself. But when Tina pressed him to tell all, he said: 'What a pity that I'm not a policeman any more, it's like worms crawling out of the foundations!'

Poor Fabian, having all this aggro, and all because he was Tina's fiancé. Strange men trying to entice him away from her, but once again the Russians were on the wrong track! They might have had better luck with 'dollybirds'.

Fabian was a real 'he-man', six foot three and all muscle and brawn. When they got back to Tooting Bec and unlocked his door, the phone rang. Just two short rings, then cut off. This was to happen every time, when they arrived. It was like saying, 'We know where you are!'

Fabian got fed up with it and said, 'Look baby, the devil is a busy man, the trick is to spot him!'

Anyway, he changed the number and went ex-directory. Little did they know that it was a wasted exercise, until one Saturday, Tina suggested a spring-clean. Together they shifted a heavy double wardrobe to discover a peephole through to next door. Most likely there was a listening device as well.

It was a private house, where the landlord lived upstairs and had three other tenants apart from Fabian, who rented the front room with a shared kitchen. The man next door was a newcomer, and was seldom seen, and he didn't use the kitchen. Most likely he lived on take-aways or ate out.

That discovery was the final straw. Fabian decided there and then to forget the spring-cleaning; he was moving elsewhere!

The following day, a Sunday, they set off to Balham. Fabian got a room on the top floor of a house, facing the back garden. It was a large family house, owned by friends of his with young children, and no other tenants. After the move, no further hassles raised their ugly heads. So Fabian could concentrate on his studies, specialising in company law, taxation, contracts and torts.

As for Stella, she wasn't investigated, and found the whole thing rather exciting. Tina had suggested that perhaps it was unwise to go everywhere together, but Stella would hear

47

none of it. She would be with her through thick and thin! As for the excitement, Tina didn't see it quite like that, but then again Stella didn't have 'a star part' in the play like Tina, and felt fear in more than a few situations. But she could take heart from the knowledge that the British Secret Service was keeping tabs on her for her own protection.

Yet there was that fear that the other side might get to her first.

Fabian had lots of mates at the law courts and in his neighbourhood. However, the saga surrounding their lives they kept secret and avoided discussing it too often. They carried on normally. If they had told anyone in their circle about their lifestyle, none would have believed them, or else thought that they had cracked up, on the road to total insanity. As for Stella, she wanted to go dancing at the Café de Paris, and got permission from Fabian that Tina could go with her, provided that they didn't go in the evening, nor get up to any mischief!

But there soon appeared other mischief-makers; newcomers to their old crowd, to dance with both girls and whisper sweet nothings in their ear!

From the British camp, there was one man who wasn't much of a dancer and yet he was always there, perhaps to keep an eye on Tina?

Usually it was just the one dance together, and in no time Tina realised that he was from MI5. Being a bit of a flirt, she was merciless in mickeytaking and nicknamed him a 'foxhound'! But the man was a true professional. He didn't try to get familiar; if anything he wanted to keep his distance, just giving sly hints as to who was who. Suddenly, there appeared some great dancers from the Eastern Bloc. There was one particular man who claimed to be from Iran and was working as a lawyer at their consulate.

But Stella soon found out that he was staying in some grotty bed and breakfast hotel in Earl's Court, because she rang the number given to her by him. Tina's senses by then were honed to smell a rat, and it just didn't add up. Meanwhile Tina rang the consulate and asked for Mr Azis Sarif, who worked there. As she suspected, there was no such person on their payroll.

The 'foxhound' didn't give much away, but he knew him to be an agitator, and he had in fact addressed a crowd at the Speakers' Corner the previous Sunday. Azis invited both girls to a Persian restaurant after the dance had finished.

The food and service were very good, and the patron and staff were very friendly towards him, unless this was just their custom with a countryman. But when they came out of the restaurant, walking along with their arms linked, hoping to hail a taxi, there was danger close at hand: a blue Volkswagen car, with three Arab-looking men inside drove straight at them, mounting the pavement. It came like a bat out of hell; luckily all three managed to jump clear into a shop doorway. Tina's first reaction was that they had tried to run her over but she was proved wrong in her theory. Azis was shaking and swearing that the Iraqis in the car were his arch enemies, and best to avoid!

After this incident, Tina and Stella avoided Azis as well; since he proved to be an imposter.

Some weeks later, when Tina asked the 'foxhound' about him, his answer left an element of doubt: 'Ah, Mr Sarif, we gave him a lift, took him around the Hammersmith roundabout a few times; and he hasn't been seen since!'

Well, that roundabout leads to the flyover towards Heathrow Airport; was that what the man was trying to say in 'secret service speak'?

Looking back to all those years ago, Tina was almost positive; that none of the crowd, not even 'All-Bran' were aware of the high drama connected to Tina at Café de Paris.

There was a very nice manager for eighteen years, who from time to time handed her free tickets, 'with compliments of

Mecca', saying with his cute smile: 'We do like to see you around!' Perhaps the 'foxhound' had taken a liking to the place too, and wanted to do his job there, rather than elsewhere.

16

At the club Tina was studying into the early hours of the morning, many a night preparing for her final exams, which she sat at three different centres. All were three-hour papers which she took at the Old Kensington Town Hall, the Royal Horticultural Hall in Victoria and a synagogue in North London. She obtained her diplomas while still at the club.

Around that time there was a rather unusual booking. One afternoon, the club secretary himself, rather than the manager, was knocking on Tina's door, when she had just finished her lunch shift. He had taken a booking for a private dinner party at short notice. It was to be for eighteen people from the Russian embassy. He looked ill at ease, asking Tina to work that evening in the private function room and to observe the service with the head waiter and wine waiter. She wasn't at all keen, but when the secretary informed her that it was a special request by a member of the club who was hosting the party, Tina relented and agreed to do it.

There was a rather tense atmosphere, even before the guests arrived. Tina was straightening the place cards when the usually affable head waiter, Mr Haines remarked, 'I expect that you know them all?'

Tina replied, 'Chance would be a fine thing!'

There was one man in particular who was constantly calling her over for something or other. Tina wasn't quite sure, but had a feeling that she had seen him before on board the ship. Was it, perhaps, Michael Khalinin?

The function room had rather tall french windows, leading to the patio. One of the women guests asked Tina to open one, as she found the room too hot. She tried, but the frame appeared to be stuck, although the catch turned. It had expanded from condensation; cold outside and heating inside. The lady in question got up herself, putting her shoulder against the frame; with wood splintering, it gave way and opened.

As the two of them were away from the table and the others, she made a peculiar remark to Tina. 'And you are supposed to be so strong?'

Tina replied, 'But obviously not strong enough!'

All eyes were on her during the dinner, it was like being on show rather than waitressing. Tina figured that someone wasn't pleased, that she remained at the club and kept her cool. She could almost read their thoughts. 'What does it take to rattle that woman; a cannon ball or dynamite?'

Upon this Tina decided that she wasn't easily cowed and acted as a 'lady of the house', and the lot of them were dining under her roof!

When it was all over she was rather pleased with herself, thinking: 'Well, you cannot please everyone all of the time!'

Soon she was to leave the club, but hadn't as yet made any definite plans. A few months earlier she had met casually an Italian girl, called Gina, at Café de Paris, and she had informed her that she worked as a waitress in Earl's Court.

One morning, whilst clearing up after breakfast, one of the waiters said to Tina that there was a call for her on the public phone; a coinbox for staff in the basement. Tina wondered, 'Who can it be at this time of the day?' A man's voice introduced himself as Maurice Collier, and said that he had heard lots of good things about her from Gina.

He was a second headhunter, and there was to be many more over the years. He was offering Tina a job, either at the hotel or in one of his tenement houses, as a housekeeper.

Arrangements were made to meet at his apartment near Marble Arch. Tina informed him that she would bring her best friend Stella along to suss him out!

He laughed, saying that he too would have backup on sussing – his wife!

Tina liked Mrs Collier on sight, although they weren't young, but in their sixties. Stella and Mr Collier didn't see eye to eye. He was saying how he was so keen on Finnish girls, because they were such hard workers and trustworthy; anyway he had too many Irish!

Stella, being one, got the hump!

It was arranged that Tina would start at the hotel, and would have a flatlet in one of his properties in Harrington Gardens; back to her old beat!

Fabian helped her with moving and met the Colliers. Tina no longer visited him, as she would have felt embarrassed staying overnight in a family house, so he did the visiting instead.

Tina worked long days, also doing reception duty and had no time for tea-dancing for quite some time.

After a year, she felt that she had no time to call her own and decided to move on and become self-employed.

17

She met a lady of property, Mrs Dalton, and her secretary Eva Walters, whom she mainly dealt with. It was another property company, which included a posh restaurant near Piccadilly Circus. Tina took her money from rents and bought stamps from a post office for her insurance cards. She was to do the lettings, collect rents and all monies from meters, gas, electric and phoneboxes, and see to the upkeep, maintenance and security of the property.

Firstly, she moved to a house in Knightsbridge, near Hyde Park Corner. It was a five-storey building which had no lift. Most of the tenants were young, singles and couples; a very 'with it' sort of crowd, except for one married couple, who turned up and were very interested in the front room on the first floor.

The ground floor was leased out for shop premises. Mr and Mrs Ramsden were over sixty and didn't quite fit in. But they had such a plausible story, wanting to live in Knightsbridge to be close to their dear friends. Tina was in two minds whether to take them on, but decided that they would be quiet next-door neighbours to herself, facing the rear of the building. And yet, they looked almost shabby, and their car was an old banger, running on a shoestring! Her second concern was how they would manage to pay the rent. Mrs Ramsden was pleased to inform her that although sixty-five, her husband was in full-time employment, working at a garage. She didn't work but would be shopping, cooking and visiting the mentioned 'dear friends'.

All went well for a while, Mrs Ramsden was very tidy in the shared kitchen, and stayed out long hours during the day. On her return she was always coming back from Harrods. Tina found it peculiar that she didn't have any shopping bags from the store. Reading her mind, Mrs Ramsden pointed out that she couldn't afford to shop there, but sat around for hours listening to gossip! She had a prominent scar on her left cheek, which was more obvious in cold weather. Tina asked her about it; had she been in an accident? After hesitating she replied, 'No, it wasn't an accident, but done deliberately when travelling through Red China.'

Tina didn't want to know any more, and turned their conversation to cooking. The husband was like a mouse, seldom seen or heard.

Another thing that struck Tina as strange was that they didn't receive any mail. Nor visitors, no 'dear friends' came to call! Tina couldn't put her finger to what it was, but felt uneasy. She should have heeded her first suspicion that they simply didn't fit in. Suddenly, Mrs Ramsden's attitude changed and she became sarcastic about Fabian staying overnight. And she didn't see a wedding band on Tina's finger, unlike her good self!

This attitude from a tenant didn't go down too well, since Tina was in charge, she had keys to all the rooms and self-contained flats on upper floors. Knowing the Ramsdens to be out, she went to check their room. All was neat and tidy, but there were so few possessions for an elderly couple. Next, the wardrobe; not much there either, except a shock to the system: a double-barrelled shotgun!

Tina hailed a taxi to the nearest police station and explained about the gun and the odd couple. She got a lift back in a police car and when they arrived the Ramsdens were home. The police went to question them, and soon escorted them to their car, carrying the gun away.

The following day the police were back to oversee them

clearing out, and noticed a listening device in the connecting wall to Tina's flat. She advised the sergeant to get in touch with MI5, they would be able to enlighten him.

He had such a sad look on his face, saying: 'I already have and learned quite a lot about the Ramsdens!'

Tina asked him to tell her as much as was possible in his position. She learned that Mrs Ramsden was Russian born, although the husband was English. They had a run-down cottage in Hertfordshire, and had no need to rent a room in Knightsbridge, except that Mrs Ramsden was paid to undertake such a mission. They seemed to be down on their luck. The police saw them out, and Mrs Ramsden hung her head in shame at being found out when she handed the two sets of keys to Tina.

No wonder that they had so few possessions, when they had a home in the country. The devil sure turns up in most unexpected guises, and is not particular regarding age or gender. Tina promised herself to be extra vigilant, but carry on, as it was all in a day's work!

She didn't mention any of the unusual goings on, since that incident on board the ship, although she exchanged letters with mama on a regular basis. She didn't want to worry her, especially when mama had recently had a mild stroke. Thankfully, she had fully recovered, but had to take pills to ward off a heart attack.

The next tenant for the front room was a smart redhead, claiming to be a fashion designer. Soon there was a constant stream of deliveries of boxes and bags, and collections of the same. Tina soon learned the truth, that Mrs Mueller was in fact only an alteration hand, making minor changes to designer wear. Thus she was using her room as a workshop. When Tina went to check, she saw an industrial sewing machine and garments all over the place.

She confronted Mrs Mueller and reminded her that she rented the room for residential use only, not commercial.

The woman was full of excuses, being strapped for cash and having to combine her workplace with her living accommodation. Tina reminded her that she was taking liberties, and had to stop her business activities or move out.

However, she was indifferent, and carried on, but she didn't reckon on what Tina would get up to until the woman towed the line!

Having ignored her warnings, Tina sneaked in to remove fuses from powerpoints. Thus, she couldn't operate the machine nor use an iron. But Tina always made sure that she was within the law, as the woman still had electricity for lights and the kitchen to use.

Being older, she expected to have her way, and went to a rent tribunal. A man called to check up on the situation. When told that she didn't have a leg to stand on she withdrew her claim for harassment and scarpered! 'Good riddance!' was Tina's verdict.

Why was she so unlucky in her lettings for that one room, when the rest of the tenants were as good as gold? Third time lucky, she hoped, and let it to a quiet businessman with no further hassle!

Having dealt with tenants, customers, tradesmen, builders and staff all those years, she regarded herself a fair judge of character. But where human nature is concerned, there is no foolproof formula. It can be fickle, unpredictable, scheming or prone to outright lying. The only answer was to be on guard, if she was to keep an upper hand.

Stella remained at the club, but missed Tina so much that she would pop over three or four evenings a week to watch television together. At the end of the evening, she would doze off and ask to stay overnight. Tina had an armchair that opened up into a narrow but comfortable bed. Fabian stayed one or two nights a week, but was privileged to share the bed. Being such a hunk, the chair wouldn't have been adequate.

The head chef at the club was an Italian chap called

Giuseppe, but Tina and Stella called him Papa. He got into a habit of sending Tina goodies from the kitchen. Stella always arrived with a small basket. They would snack on cold cuts, salads and sandwiches, while watching late films on TV.

Mrs Dalton, the proprietor of the building, plus a few others in Kensington, appeared to be very prim and proper, but Tina soon learned different! She had been married four times and had six children, all still living at home, the youngest one being only six.

Tina met his nanny, from whom she learned that there was no husband at the present time, but a boyfriend. He was an ex-cop, turned private investigator and Nanny Susan added that whenever a black silk nightie was left atop her employer's bed, that was the night when the investigator 'got his oats'.

Shaun, a carpenter and handyman, was engaged to Susan. He shared digs with two other lads somewhere in south London, whereas Susan lived in, and although it was a large house it was crowded, with nine people, including a live-in boyfriend of the eldest daughter!

They soon started visiting Tina on Sundays, their only day off work, telling her stories about Mrs Dalton, and making eyes at one another. It dawned on her that the 'poor blighters' had nowhere to do their courting, although they were to be married soon.

As they were so informative and hardworking, Tina offered them the use of her small flat on Sunday afternoons. She would go out with Stella for five hours or so, either dancing or sunbathing by the Serpentine.

Fabian didn't call till Sunday evening and then would be closer to the city for Monday morning.

The secretary, Eva Walters, gave Tina two telephone numbers, should she need to get in touch. One was her home number, and the other wasn't an office phone but a casino in Knightsbridge!

18

Looking back, those were good times socially and on the work front. Tina could plan her hours at will, which gave her a feeling of great freedom. Although she was called upon at odd times, when someone was locked out, or had a coin stuck in a meter and was left in the dark or without heating. After less than a year this situation was to change. On one winter's morning, there were three burly men at her door before eight a.m., to cut off the gas supply. Foolishly Tina asked: 'What for?'

Her initial reaction was that they were working on the mains outside. But one of them enlightened her: 'Why, because the bill hasn't been paid after the final reminder!'

Tina had to explain that she didn't own the property, but simply managed it, and that all the bills went to a house in Kensington. She couldn't possibly leave her tenants without heating, so she rang Eva, but to no avail.

At the time Mrs Dalton was abroad, and out of bounds for any contact. Tina then asked the tough guys how much the outstanding bill was for. When told, she couldn't meet it. But luckily she hadn't banked the rent monies on Friday, as usual, so she offered to pay a third in cash in return for an official gas-board receipt. The men were satisfied with this arrangement and the gas supply was left untouched.

About a week later Eva Walters turned up unexpectedly to put Tina in the picture regarding Mrs Dalton's financial difficulties. It soon became evident that none of the bills had been met. Her suggestion was to sell the remaining lease, fast!

Was there any chance that Tina could find a private buyer, rather than advertise the sale? She had already passed on all the details to Mrs Dalton's solicitors, regarding the asking price and conditions of the lease. If successful, Tina would get a commission, rather than an estate agent taking their percentage.

So, it was back to Café de Paris, this time to conduct some business and combine it with dancing.

Tina's friend Max, a freemason, had introduced her to a good friend of his called Melvyn, some years earlier. Melvyn was a property developer, and had his offices in the City, and he often had his 'right-hand man/accountant' in tow, carrying a briefcase. Upon hearing Tina's proposition over a cup of coffee on the balcony, he showed great interest in the matter. At the close of the afternoon dance, he offered Tina a lift to view the house, driving no less than a silver Bentley! According to him, the building was well maintained, but as there was no lift it wouldn't suit his portfolio. However, he knew of two brothers on the lookout for a residential property near their patch. Seemingly they owned two guesthouses near Sloane Square. He promised to send the brothers to nose around in a day or two.

Melvyn was a man of his word, and Tina escorted the brothers around the house. They decided on the spot to buy the lease. Tina gave them the address and the phone number of solicitors to contact.

Mrs Dalton was still abroad, and remained out of the country for three months. Eva was occupied at the casino, watching her chips spin on a roulette wheel! Which left only Tina to hold fort, while the sale was concluded speedily. There was a small house in Lancaster Road in Kensington where she was able to transfer some of her tenants. The others were passed on to the new proprietors, the Goldberg brothers, as a going concern.

Tina drew up an inventory of the furniture, cookers,

fridges, curtains and bedding, and handed over all the keys. Late that evening, Shaun came with a van to move her to another house in Kensington High Street. It was of similar size and period, solid but old-fashioned. Once again the ground floor front was sub-leased as shop premises and therefore the entrance was from an alleyway at the rear, leading to Wrights Lane.

The rooms were bare, as it was a vacant possession. Shaun had already started work in some of them, painting and laying new carpets.

To start with Tina's living arrangements were very primitive, but at least she had hot water and electricity. She got plumbers in to do some work in the bathrooms and to install two shower units. Telephones and coinboxes were also installed on a rental basis.

Next, she was busily measuring for curtains and nets, which she bought. Shaun was helping with rails and wires, hooks and runners.

At the time there was a market for secondhand furniture in Hammersmith, called 'The Junk City', where Tina found some great bargains: solid pine beds, chests, tables and wardrobes. Although she wasn't spending her own money she was always economical, and had an eye for 'value for money', and what was practical and hardwearing for new tenants yet to come.

When all was set up ready for letting, Tina put an advert in the *Evening Standard* and soon had a queue at the back door.

When the house was full, her life became easier again. When Mrs Dalton arrived to see the operations she was well pleased, and even more so on learning about the weekly cashflow!

A few months before moving away from Knightsbridge, out of the blue, Maurice Collier turned up on a pretext to borrow some black bags for rubbish. One of his housekeepers had run out, and they were too dear to buy at the shops. He always got them from wholesalers, but had forgotten to place an order! The real reason was that he wanted Tina back, and was trying to find fault with her present working conditions. After a while Tina turned around saying: 'How come, that you are such a sod, when your wife is so nice?'

He didn't even take offence, knowing only too well that what Tina said was a statement of fact.

After the scenario with the gas men, Fabian had called with great news. He had been offered a position in Jamaica, not Trinidad, by the British Council. It was a post that he dearly wanted to accept. Tina was disappointed that Canada was no longer on the agenda. So was his brother Arthur, who was well established there as a civil engineer. She didn't want to live in the Caribbean, and at such a short notice leave Stella and a few other close friends. So, she came to the decision that she would stay in London.

Fabian felt let down, but was determined to go. Tina returned his ring and wished him well with his career.

The next day, he came back, just to make sure that she really meant it. Tina had a one-track mind; so indeed she did. With tears and hugs they parted, never to meet again, and yet they had shared so much, and not only the closeness and happiness. So, the upheaval of the move and extra work and planning came as a welcome relief. She got stuck in and had no time for regrets.

Mr Collier was very streetwise. Tina was to learn later that he went cruising in one of his three cars along Park Lane and Sussex Gardens in the small hours of the night, picking up young 'dollybirds'. Tina once referred to his nocturnal capers: 'Just like a rat scavenging, when the city sleeps!

He knew that Tina had no sympathy for him, so he played clever. She was still living out of boxes and suitcases in Kensington, when her bell rang at ten p.m. one Sunday evening. She was really surprised to see Mr and Mrs Collier standing there in the pouring rain.

He knew that Tina would be hospitable when Mrs Collier was around. They had come headhunting for the second time around!

Tina promised to consider their offer, but for the time being she was tied up with workmen getting the house ready for letting. When she had done all that, Mrs Collier rang her, asking if she would please help them out for old times' sake, saying that her husband was in bed with a slipped disc and a broken nose. An osteopath had just left, and she had more on her hands than she could cope with alone. The housekeeper had run off in a fright, because one of the tenants had attacked Mr Collier with a pair of scissors, and all because Mr Collier had asked for the rent! The tart in question had been arrested for theft and grievous bodily harm.

This time Tina was ready to step in and sort out all Maurice's cockups. She had a lucrative business going for Mrs Dalton, and felt short-changed on her commission for acting as a middleman in the sale of the other property.

The Colliers' property accommodated some fifty tenants. There was a good sized flat for the housekeeper which although in the basement, was quite airy, having a courtyard leading to a well-maintained and leafy communal garden.

When she first came to England, Tina had found it very strange that people lived in basements, as this didn't occur in Finland. Farmhouses didn't have basement areas at all, and highrise blocks in towns and cities had them for communal uses, such as storerooms, laundry facilities, saunas and incinerators. No doubt this was due to the different climate, and severe frosts during winters.

Tina soon found out that some of the current tenants were prostitutes that Mr Collier had picked up on his cruising around and installed there. The one that attacked him was in fact 'the madame', a former air-hostess in possession of two passports, one American, the other Australian.

On learning all this, Tina felt disgusted to be part of such a household, and determined to clear them out one way or the other. She visited Maurice, sitting by his bedside, since he was laid up, and taking instructions for the forthcoming court case.

He asked Tina to present the case for prosecution on behalf of Kenton Askew Ltd. Was Tina qualified enough to handle it? He really didn't want his solicitors getting involved with all the details. Yes, Tina could see it through for a nice 'backhander', but not just for the asking.

Firstly she got two CID chaps from the local station to keep watch of the door, to see how many clients called on the madame. This was to be valuable evidence against her. Meanwhile she was threatening Tina saying, 'Who the hell do you think you are?'

'You will soon find out!' was her reply.

She felt that it would have been beneath her to get into an argument or confrontation with someone of such 'low life'.

The hearing was at a magistrates' court, and a number of tenants followed Tina to see the outcome of it. The case was referred to a crown court, where the madame was sentenced to three years' imprisonment, to be served at Holloway prison, where she had prior to the hearing been on remand.

The rest of the tarts, a total of eight, disappeared 'as mist from grass'! Soon after the case, she proceeded to select her own tenants, and run a respectable house. A limo pulled up as Tina was letting one of the prospective applicants out of the front door.

It was 'a topman' from the local police station, calling to thank Tina for clearing the whole area of prostitutes. He was very happy to deploy his men in more rewarding aspects of policework.

As Fabian had taken off to Jamaica, Tina was footloose and fancy free again. It was Melvyn who stepped in to fill the gap, but not as a boyfriend in the true sense of the word. He was so worldly-wise that she saw him as a father figure, and great company. They often met at the Café de Paris for a tea-dance, where she met the rest of his gang. They had many a dinner party at an Italian restaurant in Soho, usually celebrating someone's birthday, and the Jewish New Year was one long party, Melvyn always footing the bill. At the end of the evening, he would put Tina in a taxi and pay the driver to take her home safely.

Melvyn looked so distinguished, his manners and appearance were such that he could have just stepped out of a military academy or Savile Row tailors. One simply couldn't fault him in any way. These meetings petered out when Tina started courting her husband to be. However, in later years, she had a few more meetings with Melvyn before he moved to Monte Carlo as a tax exile!

Tina was always very concerned about the upkeep and maintenance of a property. She didn't mind getting her hands dirty, she was used to that from a very young age, mucking at the farm. Especially before the autumn rains and storms came, she would go up on the roof and balconies to check and clear any leaves and debris from the gutters and drains to avoid any leaks and water damage to the interior. On one particular sunny autumn day, she was high up with a bucket, handbrush, broom and dustpan, clearing a gutter when she noticed a man on the opposite side watching her with great interest. No, not from MI5 nor KGB; he was another property tycoon, with his Bentley parked close by!

His portfolio was hotels and hostels. Soon after that, when Tina was putting out some rubbish bags for collection he came over to speak to her saying, 'How come a nice girl like you is doing so much for an old crook like Mr Collier? Why not come across to my office, maybe we can change all that.'

'Yet another headhunter!' Tina said to herself.

As they were talking, Mr Collier pulled up in his maroon Jaguar and shooed the rival away. 'Stop poaching my staff!'

It was clear that the pair of them were not the best of friends, to say the least!

Tina never got around to popping over to the rival tycoon, though she spoke to him occasionally. She remained working for the Colliers for a total of three and a half years. She was kept on the hop, as after the first year she had taken over the management of three other houses in the Notting Hill area. Most were bedsits for young people, working and students, but a few self-contained flats as well.

She kept hearing some strange remarks about Mr Collier. When one of the regular handymen called in to do some repairs he asked her whether she knew anything about the infamous affair of Ruth Ellis and Mr Collier's involvement in the headline-making scandal.

No, Tina didn't know anything of the sort, but was sure to find out, once and for all! She rang *The News of The World* archives and asked for a copy of that story, published some seventeen years earlier. They were very efficient, and the two-page article soon arrived. Tina read it with great apprehension. The news wasn't just headlines in England but internationally.

As is documented, Ruth Ellis was the last woman in this country to be hanged in Holloway prison in 1955. The restaurant in Knightsbridge where she often met her lover, the man she shot dead, was part-owned by Mr Collier. Furthermore, the house where she lived in Kensington was one of Mr Collier's properties, rented out to prostitutes at sky-high rents.

Now that Tina knew the whole story of his shady past she was going to give him 'hell' in her own way! She had learned from the start that Mr Collier was an undischarged bankrupt. As a result, she shouldn't take too many cheques for rent. A few that she had accepted in the past had to go through her own account. Tina decided to take more of them from now on. Mr Collier noticed this from bookkeeping, as was her aim. But she simply made out that times were changing, people didn't carry cash any more. It was fashionable to carry chequebooks instead! He believed her and was a worried man. He started phoning her weekly to ask, 'How many cheques have you taken this week?'

'About forty or so!'

'As long as you don't leave the country.'

'I haven't actually booked the flight yet, but was just thinking about it!'

Tina had no more than ten or a dozen cheques at the most, but she enjoyed baiting him. His calls continued, and Tina had a stock reply until the truth dawned; that she had been taking the micky, after learning about his past. Funnily enough, he regarded it as 'fair dos'.

Whenever he was chatting with young female tenants, Tina was onto him again: 'You may own the place, but as long as I run it, no fraternising under my roof!'

When the annual shareholders' meeting came around, the Colliers were holidaying at their villa in Marbella. Tina was getting stick from numerous parties, asking about profits. She tried to pacify them by saying that as far as she knew the profits were excellent! But the Colliers couldn't be contacted, at least she didn't have their number. So the name of game was patience.

19

Tina met her husband to be at the Café de Paris, where else? It was arranged by a friend who was working for his brother's firm, which was a two-tier operation, shipping and recruitment consultancy. Jobs were all based in the Middle East, short contracts arranged in engineering and construction. Tina's husband had met the brother in Tehran.

He was already over forty, and it was his first time in England, when he joined the firm as a partner and director. Although British, his father being English, he was born abroad and joined the Royal Navy at sixteen. After serving eight years in Alexandria, he went to work for an American oil company.

They say that everything comes a full circle: There was Tina's grandfather riding the ocean waves, and so was Theo, although his ship wasn't an ocean liner, but an oil tanker in the Persian Gulf!

Tina held fast to her principles: not to live with a man until she had a wedding ring on her finger. So, Theo had to share a flat with his partner's brother until they got married on Valentine's Day in 1970. This took place at the Kensington Register Office. There was no reception, except a few invited for drinks at Tina's flat.

She was six weeks pregnant at the time, although she didn't know. A doctor had put her sickness down to having a tummy bug, until the truth dawned!

Tina had never got around to applying for British

citizenship, but decided to apply for a new passport as a British subject by marriage.

There hadn't been any major incidents for some time, although she was aware of being followed from time to time.

On this particular afternoon, she had made an appointment with her bank manager for a character reference to back up her application. A strange man followed her there. She was the last to leave the bank, as she was in the manager's office, rather than a counter customer. Someone actually came to lock the door after her. The same man was waiting outside and stalked her all the way home.

It felt so creepy; Tina expected a bullet in her back or a jab from a poisoned brolly at any time!

When she got home, she wondered whether she wasn't meant to get hold of a British passport after all. She sat down with a cup of coffee, and put pen to paper to express her melancholy.

Sweet Memories

As I think of my homeland,
looking back to the past;
childhood so sweet, it couldn't last.

I remember the springtimes,
when snow was melting,
aided by showers,
which were pelting.

Then the green grass,
pushing through,
and singing of blackbirds and cuckoos!

Sweet memories from the past,
I keep locked in my heart,

as the sun rose higher,
and the weather grew warmer
tempting the flowers,
what glory of colours;
as they bloomed through summers!

Sweet memories from the past,
I keep locked in my heart.

But the autumn turned leaves brown and yellow,
harvesting time; cool, but mellow,
turning to winter with snow and ice,
so much to offer; for skiing and slides.
What a glorious scene, and blinding sun!
In contrast of snow,
so clean and white;
and frost so strong,
it used to bite!

Sweet memories from the past;
I keep locked in my heart.

In a foreign land, I made my home,
with the baby and husband my very own!

In the boring rain, I recall the past;
Childhood so sweet, it couldn't last,

Her old friend Gina was very helpful, and always willing to
babysit and help with the housework, as she had done that
afternoon. As she had gone home, when Tina returned, she
had a little time before starting dinner. Theo returned like
clockwork at six p.m., expecting a three-course meal ready
on arrival. Baby Paul was sleeping in the nursery, which Theo
had converted very nicely from a storeroom when Tina was
still at the maternity hospital.

After putting her thoughts down on paper, she began to get angry, questioning all the whys and wherefores, saying to herself: 'I have never done a bad turn to anyone, paid my way, never committed a crime, not even a parking offence. It's five years since I sailed home on that ship, and walked into a trap. Enough is enough; it's got to stop!' But she calmed down, and decided to wait until her application was approved.

20

After her wedding, Tina jokingly wrote to mama: 'I have something in common with the Queen; like her Philip, my husband is half-Greek, and we all live in the same neighbourhood, in Kensington!

But she knew that mama wasn't fooled, no matter how she glossed it over. Her life wasn't a bed of roses. Furthermore, Tina felt that mama was secretly disappointed that she had let a man like Fabian get away. But she wouldn't say anything. Tina had made her bed and had to lie in it, hard as it was.

Tina had met an American lady, Lysette, who had recently taken a lease from Grosvenor Estates for an apartment in Eaton Square. She had been a top model living in Paris with her first and very wealthy husband. On coming to London, she had sold one of her diamond rings to set up her new husband in business, and he had opened a small factory making plastics. He too was American, and younger than Lysette. He became a stepfather to James, who was twelve at the time and at boarding school.

Lysette was a good cook and often gave dinner parties to new friends connected with fashion and the art world. She asked Tina to help out with her very first housewarming party, to serve food and drinks.

She stayed overnight on a few occasion in Eaton Square, but due to her commitments had to stay at home and carry Lysette's Pekinese dog, St Clair, in a basket everywhere. That species of dog has very short legs and they don't like going walkabout. After these dinner parties, Tina and the young husband would clear up and wash the dishes. Lysette wouldn't immerse her lovely hands in dishwater! She was truly beautiful and a focus of every gathering.

She had a large wardrobe, and some of her clothes fitted Tina perfectly, as she was still only nine and a half stone, although taller.

For her help she got some of Lysette's exclusive designer wear. But when she moved to Kensington, Lysette was at a loss; who would she trust to house-sit and look after St Clair; could Tina find her a replacement?

Yes, of course she would!

Faithful Gina was happy to stay in Belgravia. But before that, something happened. Lysette had to go to a hospital to have minor surgery on her gums. When she returned home, she found her silver-backed hairbrush in the guestroom, with blonde hairs stuck in the bristles! She accused Tina of 'having it off' with her husband while her back was turned, fuming: 'How could you, when I thought you were my friend and worthy of my trust?'

Tina remonstrated that she got it all wrong, that she would never poach anybody's husband.

However Lysette had a reason to be suspicious about him cheating on her. Tina was reluctant to upset her, but since the matter had 'come to a head' she had no choice but to do so.

The husband's secretary slept in the apartment, although in the guestroom. Lysette wasn't having any of it, but decided to give the man a second chance. It was soon after Tina's marriage when one Sunday morning Lysette's husband, Stephen, rang her doorbell. He looked unshaven, and his raincoat could have done with a dry-clean.

Tina was baffled about him calling alone, and unexpected. He too was rather embarrassed, realising that Tina now had a husband.

He suggested that they go for a stroll. Tina soon learned

that his marriage was over. He had lived with his secretary in Chelsea, but like Lysette before her, she had kicked him out. The business had gone to the wall, and he needed Tina to put him up in the house.

Theo of course would object, and in any case all the rooms and flats were occupied. However, the man looked so dejected that Tina had not the heart to walk out on him in the street. So, she directed them to a bed and a breakfast hotel that she knew of. Very discreetly she paid for a week, handing Stephen a key to a single room, and wished him luck in the future!

The Monday following Gina called with her news: Lysette had flown home to New York and the remaining lease was snapped up by Telly Savalas for three months.

The au pair had carried in a lovely, ginger Persian kitten.

Tina also had a cat; it was a tabby called Kiu-Kiu and had been a stray, and was persistent to be taken in. Having a soft spot for animals, she had relented. Before the three months was up, once again without any warning, the doorbell rang. There stood the au pair in a floppy hat, holding a basket. Tina invited her in and with a French accent she informed her that Mr Savalas and co. were flying to Europe the same day. She had to go too, and couldn't take the kitten. Could Tina look after him for a few weeks.

She left the basket on the living room floor, with the kitten, who was called Saffron-Tartan. But no toys nor cat food!

When Theo returned from the office, he found two cats playing hide and seek, and wasn't too pleased about the newcomer. But Kiu-Kiu being young herself delighted in the company of a little playmate. And play they did. At two a.m. there was still a lot of rough and tumble, until Theo jumped out of bed, took Kiu-Kiu by the scruff and locked her in a storeroom.

Tina joked: 'You wouldn't have done that to Kojak!'

Animals are so smart; after a night being locked in, Kiu-Kiu was trying to get back into Theo's good books. Every morning she would jump on a high table in the hall and give him a peck on his cheek. Never mind the expensive aftershave! In the evenings, as soon as she heard his key in the lock, she would do the same, and kiss him welcome home, rather than Tina. After his dinner, lying down on the sofa, the cat would snooze on top of his full tummy!

21

After a few months of married life Theo decided that it was time for Tina to meet her stepson, Jamie, who was only eight years her junior. He had been sent to Geneva at the age of five to a boarding school, and had stayed there until he was seventeen.

When a party from his college came over to England during termtime, Jamie had met an unmarried mum in a Brighton disco. He fell in love, and never returned with the others. He married Jessica after a short courtship.

She was twenty-two, and Jamie had falsified his age as eighteen, otherwise he would have needed parental consent, but Theo was not informed. On his annual visit to Geneva to see his son, he learned that he was no longer at the campus, but living in Brighton, England.

'The son of a gun, he has a lot to answer for!' was Theo's reaction.

By the time they came to visit, they had been married for three years, and little Marcus was nearly four years old.

Jessica was a former 'Lucy Clayton' model, and Jamie had model looks too, and was tall, like his father. However, he sounded like a Frenchman, that being his first language. He was bilingual, but was no match for Theo who was fluent in seven languages, including Arabic.

Jamie's mother was French/Armenian, and had cheated on Theo with other captains and he was the last to know. Hence Jamie being sent abroad at the very young age.

By Islamic law he had to maintain her in the same lifestyle

for seventeen years, before obtaining a divorce. Granted by a court in Damascus, final authorisation was given by the Swiss embassy in Geneva.

He felt badly hurt, as any man would. Tina later learned that in fact it embittered him so much that he would 'turn the tables' and have it the other way round next time!

So, unwittingly, Tina ended up being the breadwinner!

She was disappointed, but had never relied on any man financially – if anything, it had been the other way round.

When she was eight months pregnant, they paid a return visit to Brighton on the August bank holiday weekend. Gina and her boyfriend, Roberto, stayed to house-sit, and feed the cats.

Tina, being very houseproud, noticed that the young couple weren't very domesticated. Neither had ever had to be concerned with domestic chores, but the main thing was that they were happy, and learning to manage a home.

22

Earlier in the summer Tina was invited to attend the wedding of Susan and Shaun. It was a church do, and the reception was held at the Milestone Hotel in Kensington High Street.

Mrs Dalton was 'on the up' financially, and she paid for it all! A very nice gesture, but both had worked for her for a number of years. Long before the wedding, Eva had invited Tina to have dinner at Mrs Dalton's restaurant near Piccadilly. The interior was rather plush, with seating all in red velvet and belly-dancers wiggling around the tables.

Not quite her cup of tea, but Tina knew that Eva had a reason to entertain her there. The restaurant was to be sold. Did Tina know of anyone who might be interested? This time she didn't want to get involved, and in truth didn't know anyone with interest or money.

Whilst courting, Theo would take Tina dancing at the Café de Paris on Saturday nights, as she had gone with Fabian before him. When Stella realised that she was soon to 'get hitched', she panicked, saying 'What am I going to do now?'

Tina advised her to register with a marriage and friendship bureau in Bond Street. And the very first introduction was to become her husband! Meanwhile, after just one meeting, Stella didn't care for Theo, saying to her privately, 'Who does he think, he is; Aristotle Onassis?'

But Tina suspected that there was some rivalry for her affections between them. However, Theo never said anything against Stella, except that he didn't quite see the two of them having anything in common.

Six months after Tina, Stella too was a married lady living a quiet life in the country. No more waitressing for her, nor need for any other occupation! Tina kept in touch for a while, the husband was a very decent chap, with a good position in the building industry.

Tina was charmed by Theo, there was something 'so international' about him, and his military carriage didn't go amiss! So, she figured that it would be safe and secure to settle down with an older man.

But there is no such a thing as a safe bet where matrimony is concerned.

23

Tina was 'on the go' from six a.m. until midnight. What with nearly two hundred tenants, there was always somebody moving out or in.

She was running between the houses in Notting Hill and in Kensington, to show applicants around for viewing. She had a difficult time with her pregnancy, suffering for the first and the only time in her life from high blood pressure. She ballooned to twelve stone, with water retention, and twins were forecast until the last minute!

When Theo visited her at the maternity ward, they agreed that the two cats were so pampered that they would be jealous of the new baby, and therefore be too risky to keep on.

Every day Theo promised to find them good homes. But when Tina returned home, the cats came to greet her, sniffing very suspiciously about her bundle. She reminded Theo that on that very day they had to go. By then he had become so attached to them, he kept postponing the inevitable.

Kiu-Kiu was collected by Sheila from a nearby house, and Gina took Saffron-Tartan to Roberto's bedsit close by.

All Tina asked of them was to be kind and feed them well, lest they ran back. Kojak and co. never returned to claim their kitten, by which time it was a fully grown cat. To this day he is indebted to Tina for six months' supply of cat food.

Tina had a private GP locally, and what a caring doctor he was; over seventy and couldn't retire due to popular demand for his services by his long-standing clients. Tina's blood pressure was reaching dangerous levels. One day she had been hanging up curtains in one of the flatlets upstairs, standing on a high table. When she came to, she found herself flat on the floor, overturned table on top, and a bump on the head. These dizzy spells concerned her, so she went to see the doctor.

He asked her about her home life and her husband's occupation, promising to arrange for some tests to be done. This was Friday afternoon. The following Sunday morning he called at the house unexpectedly to see Theo, and lecture him!

'What kind of a man are you? Your wife is only twenty-eight, with a blood pressure so high that she might drop dead any time! I have taken the liberty to book her into a health farm in Suffolk, two weeks' stay for a complete rest. And you sir are going to pay for it, seeing as you can well afford to!'

For the first time ever Tina saw him gobsmacked, and meek as a little boy. He didn't object to what the good doctor had arranged.

Paul was only three months old, and Tina felt terribly guilty about leaving him, and yet she was looking forward to some rest; after all, she was obeying doctor's orders! She enjoyed all the attention and pampering, even the fasting, to get rid of the extra weight that she had gained. So much so that it became a lifetime habit.

Tina would book a fortnight's stay every five years from then on!

Theo rang her daily asking when she was coming home and saying that the baby was crying for her. But Tina stayed on until two days before Christmas, when the clinic was to be closed for the holidays.

On her return, Theo prepared T-bone steaks with jacket potatoes and was crestfallen when Tina could only eat a few mouthfuls.

Furthermore, he was shamefaced when Tina learned that it had taken three people to do her work! Small wonder that she had suffered from high blood pressure!

Theo had stayed home the whole time. Gina had been every day from dawn to dusk to look after the baby and cook and clean for Theo!

And Mrs James, the cleaner, who did the public areas, stairs, landings and bathrooms Monday to Friday had been working seven days a week!

24

Tina hadn't been to Finland since 1967, and couldn't arrange it for some time to come, what with all her commitments. When she felt her energetic self again, and got her British passport in the new year, she arranged for Gina to babysit again. She had a job as a breakfast waitress in a hotel, but was available during the day.

Tina told her that she had some important business to take care of in Westminster the following afternoon.

Theo wasn't in the know about her decision. Tina paid a visit to Scotland Yard, giving her name at reception. When asked what the matter concerned, Tina replied, 'Protection,' and that she wished to see 'the top man' at Special Branch. A phone call was made to someone, and after a short wait she was escorted to a plush office on one of the upper floors.

She was seated opposite a man, and talk about handsome! Tina felt that she had come face to face with 007 himself! But she came straight to the point saying, 'You have a file on me?'

'Yes, we do.'

Tina then expanded on some incidents that had given her concern in the past. 'But after five years looking over my shoulder, it has to end. Or else, give me a badge and teach me to shoot, and I will join you!'

'We have only done it for your protection,' replied 007.

However, he promised to inactivate her file. When Tina was at the door ready to leave, he remarked as an afterthought, 'They never give up; once they have gone so far.'

'Thanks for telling me, but I will take my chances,' replied Tina. Stepping into the sunshine and heading for St James's tube station, she said to herself, 'Wow, what a guy,' comparing him to a Sumatran tiger poised to pounce; all that unleashed power! An ex-marine most likely, if not SAS-trained.

But his word was his bond. Perhaps he had put a word to the 'other side' as well, to 'give over', and it all ended.

And yet Tina was in the dark about so much of it.

No wonder that they call it the Secret Service!

Theo paid the bill for the health farm, as the good doctor had ordered, but only because he had been fortunate enough to have a small win on the football pools, which just about covered it!

Sometime later Tina asked him for money to buy a new dress. Theo looked her straight in the eye, saying with a voice like ice, 'If you want to buy a dress, go to the bank!'

After that, Tina was too proud to ever ask again. It was the same with household expenses. Whenever he shopped for food, he would present a receipt, expecting to be refunded.

'How deceiving can first appearances be?' Tina asked herself.

Thus the resentment set in, and she began to regard her husband as a non-paying guest.

The measure of their social life wasn't very exciting either; Sunday outings in the park, and sometimes a lunch. A visit to a theatre once in a blue moon. Occasionally, Tina invited some old friends for drinks or Sunday lunch, which Theo would cook.

He was very experienced in culinary skills, and could prepare a very tasty dish of stuffed veal in cream sauce, and even do home-made crème caramels! But only on Sundays; if asked to help during the week, he would be really affronted and sulk for days!

During their visit to Brighton, Theo made a point of telling Jessica how little he thought of her as a wife and homemaker, saying, 'I am surprised that your cooking hasn't poisoned my son yet!'

After this, Jessica didn't want to meet Theo again, but they kept in touch with Tina. She came into town in the afternoon to shop at Harrods and pop over when Theo was at work.

Jamie used to phone asking Tina to act as a middleman, to get some money out of his dad. Tina pointed out to him that it was very unlikely to happen, since she herself didn't share in his wealth. Jamie found it hard to take in, asking, 'What does he do with his money?'

A good question! Tina herself was asking it silently, day in day out. Of course, having his suits and shirts tailor-made, and hair treatment at the barbers regularly, must have cost a pretty penny!

But he had no living expenses, no mortgage nor rates. No bills for electricity or telephone; none except fares to work.

In the Middle East he had smashed up so many company cars, losing his licence, and it had worked out cheaper to give him a full-time chauffeur.

Outwardly, they appeared to be a happy couple, as Tina didn't tell nor complain to anyone. After all she had taken her vows for better or worse. So she decided to keep her problems to herself, dealing with 'the worse'.

He might have been a good husband, had his first marriage not been such a let-down and disappointing.

Finding out about his wife sleeping with other captains, and being the last to know, had poisoned his mind to women. He was looking to take his revenge on the next one that crossed his path!

That very same woman, his first wife, telephoned Tina one afternoon, inviting herself for tea and to meet up, as she was in London for a short visit. Tina soon put her in her place, saying that her time was too limited to stretch to socialising, so sitting down for tea wasn't on her agenda!

The woman wanted Theo's help in obtaining a British passport. Tina gave her his office number, so that they could sort it out between the pair of them.

After Theo divorced her, she married two doctors in their late seventies, and unlikely to live much longer. Their demise increased her bank balance! Unlike Tina, she never had to lift a finger on the workfront. Her fourth, and to Tina's knowledge, her last, husband was an Englishman from Leicester. Having never met either, Tina felt pity for him all the same.

25

When Jamie reached the age of twenty-one, he legally adopted little Marcus. As Jessica's father felt that their marriage had solid foundations, being in the trade himself, he had a lovely bungalow built for the young couple in Hove. But Marcus had suffered from asthma from a young age, and it was getting worse. After five years of happy marriage, they had a little girl called Anne-Marie. Around this time, Jessica's doctor advised her that Marcus would benefit from a warmer climate. So, the following year, they emigrated to Australia and Tina lost touch with them.

She soon discovered another minus point to Theo's nature. He was obsessed with jealousy, expecting Tina to behave like his first wife when his back was turned. He never even went to a pub alone, so he could keep an eye on Tina. On the surface, one couldn't fault him: no drinking, womanising, gambling, nor wife-beating, and yet Tina felt as if she were under 'captain's orders'!

Most of the tenants were young, very presentable men, executives working for John Lewis or in various banks and embassies. Tina would take their rent money, and enter such transactions in the rentbooks in the hallway.

One particular evening a chap who worked for the Norwegian embassy made his usual polite small-talk ending with: 'And how is your father?'

Tina whispered, 'He is my husband, in fact!'

Theo had overhead and lectured Tina for being over-friendly, saying, 'Just take the money, and be done with it!'

That led to their first full-blown argument, with Tina saying that he lived under her roof, didn't pay any rent, nor bills, therefore was not fit to criticise! Theo sulked for days to come, and thereafter gave all the male tenants a cold shoulder, should they meet in the hallway or outside.

Next, Tina was to meet Theo's cousin Nicholas and his family, and his Aunt Betty, when they were invited for Sunday lunch at their large and well-maintained house in Middlesex.

Aunt Betty was ninety-three years old, but bright as a button! They had a very large back garden, where they sat after lunch to take their coffees. Tina was intrigued about all the wires and cables running across it into the house, and asked Nicholas what they were for.

'I have a radio up in the attic, come and see it!' he enthused like a schoolboy with a new game.

It looked like a radio station. Nicholas pushed a few buttons, and the line crackled alive. He was trying to get hold of King Hussain of Jordan on his yacht. And, sure enough, he did. The unmistakable Oxford educated elocution with deep baritone came over the wires, clear as a bell!

Well, there was a turn up for the books, and at last Tina had seen how it was done. And now it had a family connection. However, she wanted to put all that behind her and didn't linger in the attic.

Nicholas had recently retired from the British Secret Service, having been based at the government listening post in Cyprus.

'Talk about tales of the unexpected!'

26

Tina was to meet yet another member of Theo's family, Uncle Alec, who was visiting London and staying at the Grosvenor House Hotel in Knightsbridge. They were invited to have dinner with him at the hotel. As they were getting ready, Theo decided that Tina wasn't going after all. She was at a loss as to what had changed his mind. She was looking forward to it and asked him, 'Why not?'

'The bastard bedded my first wife and pinched two of my girlfriends later on. Who is to know that he won't try to pull a fast one with you as well?'

Tina felt insulted, but seeing his vengeful mood, let him go alone. The next day Uncle Alec rang Tina to say how disappointed he was at not having met her, adding, 'Why on earth did a nice girl like you marry a bastard like Theo? Did you not know that he is a black sheep of the family?'

Tina answered, 'Not exactly, but I am beginning to have my doubts and let my heart rule my head!'

She promised to meet him next year, when he would be holidaying in London. On his return from the dinner, Theo didn't look too happy, and told Tina more about his uncle.

He was a retired banker and had been a resident of Monte Carlo for twenty-seven years. He was seventy-three years old, but still sowing his wild oats, as he had recently married his fourth wife, who was only twenty-four and a starlet, having had some bit-parts in French television. It was clearly a case of marrying a sugardaddy to further her career.

When they were having their dinner the following day,

Tina was so intrigued about Alec, that she asked Theo, 'How did Alec make his millions?'

'By growing opium in Monaco!' was his answer.

Tina was flabbergasted, saying that he didn't sound one bit like a crook over the phone.

'How would you know anyway, seeing a good side in everyone!'

But no, Alec had never been a crook, he grew it for medical purposes, all perfectly legal and very lucrative! So much so, that he was able to open a private bank in Switzerland. And to this day his hobby was money, foreign coins, piled up in disused fridges, so that he could handle and play with them!

Tina wasn't sure whether this was true or not. But one thing was certain, that Alec was filthy rich. But Theo wasn't going to get a penny out of him!

Theo and Mr Collier didn't like each other one little bit. Mr Collier would drop in from time to time, watching Tina rushing about and say, 'Why did you marry a bastard like him!'

When Theo returned from his office, he learned of the visit, and got his bit in by asking, 'Why do you work for an old crook like him?'

That left her between a rock and a hard place.

Mr Collier's aim in life was to make money, and then some more, and he had no social graces whatsoever, whereas Mrs Dalton had a Cambridge education, and knew all about etiquette. Going through the bookkeeping, Mr Collier would always say to Tina that he was hungry.

'Any chance of a sandwich and a cup of coffee?'

As a rule, she would cater to his whims. On one occasion she made a sandwich with smoked salmon on brown bread.

He came back the next day all dressed up on his way to some meeting to ask, 'Have you any more of that salmon in your fridge?'

Tina was rather put out, saying, 'No.'

But he didn't believe her, and actually went to look into the fridge, only to see it there!

Tina jokingly pointed out that she wasn't exactly running a restaurant and that it was rather pricey!

But since he had especially called to have some more, she relented. But that wasn't the end of it. That same evening it was Theo's turn to look into the fridge, as he fancied a late-night snack of smoked salmon.

'What has happened to it?' he called from the kitchen.

Tina had to tell him about Maurice being on the prowl.

'I don't believe it! The man has a villa in Marbella, three cars to choose from, six properties in London! Are you telling me that he cannot afford to pay for his food?'

Tina kept her cool saying, 'One thing is clear, now I have two freeloaders on my hands!'

Theo got the hint, and said no more.

However, the next time Mr Collier announced that he was hungry, Tina had a ready reply: 'There is a very nice café up in Gloucester Road!'

He looked up, expecting her to say more.

'Captain's orders!' added Tina.

And, happily he didn't drop in quite so often from then on, which suited her just fine.

27

Although Tina hadn't been home for a few years, she kept in touch with mama, but no longer told all, only about aspects of her life that wouldn't upset her. It was as if they had a link of telepathy.

Tina would say to Theo over the breakfast: 'Can you get the mail? There is a letter from mama.'

At first, he found this very peculiar, but got used to it.

Most of the time a date of writing coincided, and their letters crossed the Channel in transit. There might have been two weeks or a whole month in between, yet it was always the same.

The night before she would dream of being back home, so the letter was just a confirmation of the news.

She now dreamed in English, and remembered when the turning point came. She had been keeping two diaries, first writing in Finish, and then translating into English. After two years she felt that the country was to become her permanent home.

During the summers, mama didn't lack for visitors. They came from as far as Helsinki, arriving on Saturday and leaving Sunday evening, with their car boot full of home-produce: fruit and veg from the kitchen garden, goats'-milk cheese, homemade lemonade, fruit juices and jams, and a chunk of smoked ham. Mama had half a pig sent to a smokehouse for six weeks from her own stock. During the summers there was a plentiful supply of cold cuts for salads and sandwiches. Oh, and the taste and texture of it; Tina has never since tasted anything like it! Mama was so versatile, she could turn her hand to anything, and be so good at it.

Sister Irene had left the bank and worked for the prison services as a clerical officer, in order to get a higher salary and longer holidays as a civil servant. Husband Ari continued to hit the bottle. The locks in the apartment had been changed. When in his cups he could be abusive. Divorce proceedings were underway, as they were legally separated.

Brother Leo remained a bachelor. He was often asked why he didn't take a wife, as it would have meant help for mama in the kitchen and the farm.

'How could I ever be sure whether they fancy me or the farm?' was his standard excuse.

Personally, Tina suspected that his real reason was self-preservation! Would matrimony alter his cushy life?

During the summer holidays the farm and the surrounding countryside was a welcome haven for Irene and the boys, Petri and Folkke, as long as they wore woollen socks or wellies in the woods and outer fields, so as not to get bitten by poisonous adders. It happened to the farm dogs occasionally, especially when they went in a pack to hunt water-rats by the reservoir.

But dogs being such a clever species, they had communicated to each other and their pals from neighbouring farms the secrets of mama's medicine bag. When bitten, usually on the face, with a swelling the size of a golfball, they ran to the house for help. Otherwise, they would have died with an hour or two.

Tina was rather finicky, but once was asked to watch. Mama lanced the affected area, and squeezed the venom out, and used alcohol as a steriliser and antidote. After a wee nap, the four-legged friends were up and running, as if nothing untoward had happened!

Only once Tina was in a situation when she had to kill an

enormous snake with a heavy fence pole. There was a wedding, followed by a barn dance in the next village. The family was invited, and Tina wanted mama to get there early in the afternoon to see the minister who would marry and bless the young couple. She volunteered to feed the animals and do the milking. Being summer, the cows were out in the pasture, where she had to go with a milk cart and heavy galvanised urns. The normally placid cows were nervous and restless. Tina looked around, and no more than a metre from her foot was the adder. Tina was terrified herself; it unnerved her, although it was quite still, and twice the size of the norm. When she hit it, little babies slithered into the grass. They were shiny black as opposed to the grey and black ziz-zag pattern of the adult. Although it was a snake, the fact that it was giving birth made her physically sick.

She sat on a bank of a bubbling brook trying to put it in perspective and give the animals time to settle down. It really was a Hobson's choice; had she not done so, then either herself or one of the cows would have got bitten. Furthermore, she was all alone, as everyone had gone to the wedding; and she was only fourteen years old!

When she finally got there, it was nearly over. All the cake and food had gone and the family came to ask why she was some three hours late. She didn't want to spoil their happy mood of revelling by saying that she had committed murder, and had been feeling sick ever since.

28

Little Paul started walking at a very early age, and needed constant supervision. When he was two years old, Tina realised that she could no longer cope with her workload. She would have needed a full-time nanny, for which the flat wasn't suitable.

And around this time she cricked her back, by moving heavy furniture upstairs. She was on strong painkillers, but it wasn't a solution. In fact she needed physiotherapy or traction for it at Guy's Hospital. She was under the care of a Harley Street specialist who was a consultant there. But she was unable to start her treatment until she had given up her job, and they moved to west London.

Also, Tina was secretly hoping that when she had no income Theo would assume his responsibility as a provider for his family. Tina herself went to view a house one evening, when Theo had returned from the office. She found it just the thing, having a large back garden and a common nearby. She came to an agreement with the landlords that she would only sign a six-month lease initially, not being sure how it would all work out. They were happy to go along with this, but regarded it as more appropriate if the lease was in her husband's name, and wanted to meet him as well.

Theo went along with the plan, except he wouldn't pay the deposit nor the first month's rent. After all, the move was Tina's idea! The only thing for it was to go to her bank and draw out a large amount of cash. It broke her heart for being so blatantly used.

By this time she had lost all her faith in 'her man' and wondered whether he would use the cash for some other purpose instead. Had it not been for the sake of little Paul, she would have kicked him out long ago.

It was a very unhappy time for Tina, as by this time she couldn't lift Paul's pushchair into public transport, and found that any stairs would trigger a sharp pain in her lower back. Only someone who has suffered a back injury, either from an accident or stress, can really know how awful it is. She has heard it compared to 'sticking a knife in your back'. She regarded it as having a paralysing effect.

Mr Collier's attitude didn't help at all. He was very upset about her leaving, blaming Theo that she was no longer a laughing, 'happy go lucky' girl, as he had first known her, but a sad woman with 'a long face'. He had a point, but by this time the long face was more to do with the pain than the misery of her situation.

Tina decided not to leave their new address, should he come after her again, but Theo's office address in the city instead.

There followed a month of struggle and heavy expenditure, as Tina needed a minicab service to take Paul to and from his nursery, and for herself, to and from the hospital twice weekly. She couldn't even claim any benefits, because of her husband's income.

One evening, Theo brought a letter which had been hand-delivered to his office premises the previous evening. Tina recognised Mrs Collier's handwriting. Inside she found a personal cheque for £500, and a short note to say that it was a thank you for all her help and hard work over the years.

It was a lot of money in 1972 and a Godsend. No doubt, Mrs Collier had long since realised that the family depended on Tina, although it was never discussed. She was so right in expressing her opinion after their first meeting that Mrs Collier was truly a nice person.

Tina's private doctor had put her on valium on top of the painkillers, to cope with it all. However, after taking them for three months, she decided that such props were not the answer, and stopped taking them. She was determined to manage 'under her own steam', and never touch tranquillisers again, come what may. She needed a clear mind to undertake drastic measures shortly.

Paul had caught an ear infection at the nursery. Her doctor came for a home visit and booked him into Westminster Children's Hospital, in a private ward. Even for this, Theo refused to pay the bill, but Tina pointed out that it was in his name and should he not comply, he was likely to face court action for non-payment. Suddenly, he had plenty of money, and settled up promptly! While Paul was at the hospital, Tina decided to tell Theo that she was running out of funds and as a result they all had to go their separate ways. She made it clear to him that she wouldn't have minded keeping a man who was poor or sick, but a man in his position had no excuse to freeload on any woman!

29

When they were courting, Theo had told her about his background. His mother had twenty-two children. The first twenty with her first, Greek, husband and two more with her second husband, who was English.

Theo's father was in the colonial services with Ministry of Agriculture and Fisheries. They had a free government house on a Greek island. His father had been very strict, to the extent that Theo got his backside tanned by a belt-buckle if he was five minutes late in joining the dinner table! However, he was looked after by a French nanny most of the day, and that was how he learned the language.

Tina found it quite extraordinary and unnatural to have that number of children; the largest family that she had known was nine children, the last two being twins.

Theo's sister Glenda was a year older than him. Tina had made a playful remark that it was no wonder that the last one in the line was a bit addled! This remark came to haunt her later on.

Tina asked him how he got on with the older brothers and sisters. His answer rather surprised her.

'I had nothing to do with them, bandy-legged monkeys!'

But he had a very close relationship with sister Glenda. At an early age she had joined the Royal Navy, and served as a Wren in Malta at the British base. Tina never met her, but her husband, who hailed from Cambridge, was a lovely man. He called to visit them in Kensington twice a year, when on business in London. Ricky Winslow-Aalton was a financier, working for the United Nations. He and the family were based in Kenya, in Nairobi for eighteen years. He brought such lovely toys, stuffed animals such as lions and giraffes for Paul. They had one son, who became a lawyer. Ricky wanted him to go to law school in England, but due to government restrictions on sending money out of the country, he had his hopes dashed. Kelvin ended up studying in Johannesburg, South Africa.

When the Afrikaaner government got into power, they asked for a transfer to another base, to live in Rome. In the early nineties Glenda moved to London to be close to Theo, who by then was retired. Ricky had passed on before her move. After three years' stay, she too passed on.

30

What Tina had to contend with for five years was rather stressful at times, being bugged and stalked. But it was 'a piece of cake' in comparison to her battles with Theo, that were to begin and go on and on!

Stella came to visit her in Ealing, when Theo was in the office, otherwise she wouldn't have come. Over lunch they talked about their 'capers' and good times, prowling in the West End, and especially at the Café de Paris. But both realised that Tina's social life had come to an end. She wasn't able to go anywhere unless Theo came too. Tina was genuinely pleased that at least Stella had picked 'a good one', and told her loyal and long-time friend just that!

Theo listened quietly while Tina explained the situation to him. She had already been to the Social Services department to place Paul in a residential nursery on a voluntary basis. Later both parents signed an agreement to pay towards his upkeep, according to their means. At first Theo said quite calmly, 'If you leave me, I will make damn sure that you lose your son for good!' He then continued to put in a few curses, as a deserved punishment. 'To suffer every illness and disease under the sun!'

Tina remained seated in her armchair by the french windows, in her nightie and bare-footed. She assumed that Theo had gone to the kitchen to make a nightcap. But she was in for a shock, because he burst into the living room holding an axe high with both hands, with a mad look in his eyes, shouting: 'You cannot leave me, because I am going to kill you first!'

Tina jumped up in a flash and ran through the dark garden, Theo close behind her. She jumped over the wall, cutting her feet badly. She looked over to see him turning back into the house. Had Tina not been so keen on sport and in regular training, she wouldn't be here to tell you this sad saga of so-called married bliss!

It was a cold night, and she was so flimsily dressed, so she had no choice but to creep back.

She found Theo slumped in his armchair, sobbing. His slippers were wet from the dew in the grass, and the axe was propped against his chair.

Tina figured that he was having a nervous breakdown, or was he addled? She was in two minds whether to call the police or a doctor. But in 1972, domestic violence wasn't taken very seriously by the police, as it is these days. Furthermore, Theo had never been violent before, and since Tina had managed to escape, she hadn't suffered any physical harm. She decided to call a doctor to give him a sedative. By this time he was crying that Tina didn't deserve someone as bad as him, that she had always been a good wife and mother. He was mad even to think that she would cheat on him.

All the same she was frightened to stay with him, not knowing which way his mood might swing. Thank God that little Paul was out of harm's way! A doctor arrived and gave him a shot in the arm, as Tina had asked him to knock him out for some twelve hours so that she, too, could get some sleep. But of all things, the doctor asked for his fee of £50.00, because he was 'a Harley Street man'!

Tina asked, 'What in God's name is a Harley Street man doing on my doorstep at one o'clock in the morning?'

'I happened to be on call!' was the answer.

It didn't add up, and Tina began to wonder whether she too had lost her marbles. But no, quite the opposite, as she had just had a darn good run in the frosty air. The doctor no doubt was good, as far as medical knowledge went, but how could he be so insensitive? Did he not observe the sorry state of affairs? Husband gibbering, an axe in the living room, Tina with bleeding feet, and the hem of her nightie wet and dirty?

As it was, she cleaned and bandaged her feet herself, and told the doctor that she would settle his fee with her GP in the morning.

She went to Kensington to do just that, and needless to say she didn't pay £50.00, nor was she asked to. In fact, the charge was £15.00.

Perhaps she should have called the police after all, as it would have been free! When Tina returned after lunch, having visited Paul in the nursery on her way to Victoria, Theo was just waking after a twelve-hour sleep. He didn't mention the night before. Tina had locked his weapon in a cupboard under the stairs with the other tools, and kept the key on her person, just to be on the safe side. She was hoping that Theo would move out that day, but no such luck; he would stay as long as Tina was there!

Tina had given notice to the landlords, although the six months wasn't quite up yet, so she would have to pay up to the agreed date. They had already realised that this wasn't a normal marriage, since Tina had sent her personal cheques for rent payments.

Two days before moving out, one of the landlords telephoned her, saying that he wanted her husband gone before they came over to check the inventory for any damage, and settle the bills. They would only deal with Tina, and regarded her man as nothing but a conman!

Tina asked him to call again in the evening and tell the same to Theo, as he wouldn't have believed her. He did too, and Theo got the message!

Tina was going to put all her household items into storage. But Theo suggested that it wouldn't cost anything to store them at his office premises, as he had enough space in the storeroom. So he left with a driver, and a full van load. It was quite a load: Paul's pram, pushchair, cot, playpen and lots of toys, all the kitchen utensils, bedding and towels, cushions, and most of Tina's clothes and shoes. She only took one suitcase and a holdall to her new position, which was a temporary measure.

Theo didn't seem to have any plans as to where he was going to live, so Tina was to use his office as a contact address.

Thank goodness that she had a deposit, otherwise she wouldn't have been able to meet the final payments: telephone, gas and electricity bills. Luckily the inventory tallied, and there was no damage or breakages. Even then, Tina was left so broke; she had hardly more than the minicab fare to Earl's Court where she had a residential post as a manageress of a sixteen-roomed bed and breakfast hotel. She really was thrown in at the deep end.

When she got to the hotel, the previous manageress and her teenaged daughter were in the reception area, with packed suitcases, and in the hurry to get away and hand the keys over. When they were gone, Tina checked the office diary to see whether there were any arrivals booked for that evening and how many rooms were occupied. There were only two vacant ones, which she filled during the late evening when people just called at the door enquiring about vacancies.

Her predecessor had mentioned that her room was a double in the basement near the kitchen. In no time, she realised that she was totally on her own. The assistant manageress had walked out.

She went to see her room, and left her luggage by an unmade bed. Then she checked the dining room and kitchen, and the contents of the fridges. She was annoyed to find the tables not cleared after breakfast; milk was turning sour in the jugs, and there were loads of dirty dishes to be washed. She came to the conclusion that there wasn't enough food for Sunday morning's breakfast. So she made a list, expecting a milkman to call, but no other deliveries on a Sunday.

As she couldn't leave the hotel unmanned, she telephoned her faithful friend, Gina, with a shopping list. She herself 'got stuck in' with washing up and changing the tablecloths, and setting them up again for the next morning's breakfast. Gina arrived around nine p.m. that evening, and helped Tina to clean the kitchen and wash the grease off the floor with a drop of bleach in hot water.

Then they cleaned Tina's room and made the bed. As it was getting late, and it seemed that Tina was going to be alone to cook and serve twenty-seven hotel guests, Gina volunteered to sleep over, sharing the double bed. She helped in the morning to get things underway. The hotel was part of a group of half a dozen small hotels, so, during the morning, Tina rang two of them, asking them to send her a couple of girls to clear the tables, make the beds and do the cleaning. She was quite firm in her request, saying that she was known 'to do the impossible', but was not one to perform miracles!

Her request was granted for Sunday and Monday only, until she employed her own staff, which she accomplished on Monday, having placed an advert in a newsagent's window. Two South American girls arrived, and would work from seven a.m. to three p.m. Tina also engaged an assistant manageress, a very capable Australian girl called Jenny, who was to live in.

The hotel was nicely furnished, with a comfortable TV lounge, but cleaning-wise it was on 'a slide', what with staff not staying put!

Tina didn't plan on staying long herself, but since she had taken over she was determined to get the place spick and span.

Since there was a Finnish lady in charge, it was more or less expected. All the rooms had a spring-clean, and the bedcovers made a trip to cleaners. The stairs and landings had a good going over with a stiff brush. Tina washed and ironed all the nets herself and while Jenny was in reception she was able to prowl on the upper floors.

But it was a shock to the system to sleep in the basement and share the kitchen after moving out from a comfortable house, so she purposely worked from seven a.m. until midnight, when she would turn off the lights and lock up. This was in order to wear herself out, so that she would fall asleep from sheer exhaustion and not pine for Paul, nor think about her home comforts too much.

She had everything running smoothly after ten days' stay. She was in the kitchen, defrosting and washing out the fridges, and at the same time supervising two carpenters who were putting up extra shelves. Suddenly, Jenny ran down the stairs calling, 'Tina, go hide! Your husband is in reception blustering about being an important man, and no wife of his should work in a cheap hotel!'

Tina had no reason to hide, and in any case she preferred to deal with matters up front. Theo was, as usual, all dressed up in a Savile Row suit, with tinted glasses and greying temples; he looked like a million dollars! But he was full of hot air, which spoiled the image. He was planning on returning to the Middle East, and Tina must go with him, if she had any sense at all. She wouldn't have to work there, as he had four servants, including a chauffeur provided with a free company house. She could play tennis and attend cocktail parties with the European community in that locality!

Tina responded that, 'Since the foundations have long since rotted, we have nothing to build on!' She asked him not to call again, as it was rather embarrassing for her; what with staff and workmen expecting fireworks.

105

'In that case,' he said, 'I will have to go with a young mistress instead!'

Tina had already turned down an opportunity of a jet-set life in Scandinavia, and enjoying sunshine in Jamaica, so the Middle East wasn't 'her cup of tea'. She intended to be poor and busy, rather than rich and idle. She felt that money earned was worth so much more in her pocket, and doing a full day's work had become a way of life for her!

31

No wonder that Theo hadn't made any arrangements when they moved out. He carried on being parasitic, expecting to be put up by Julia and Jeremy. They had visited a few times in Kensington, as Jeremy supplied him with office stationery and printing materials, and Julia was a secretary to his solicitors. He had told them a hard luck story, how Tina was a heartless bitch to kick him out!

They were very put out by his presence in their flat. Jeremy rang Tina for advice about what to do about him, as he didn't seem to be quite himself, but hellbent on revenge. In the end, he had asked his elderly father in Scotland to come over for a visit and talk some sense into the man. Nearing eighty, he had come with a Bible, telling Theo that he would find all the answers in the Good Book.

Tina herself had always regarded her faith in The Almighty as a cornerstone of her life. Whenever God himself was too busy, then there had always been some minor minion from that department to give her a helping hand. Although not much of a churchgoer, she said her prayers first thing in the morning and last thing before going to bed.

Theo was baptised as a Catholic, but before joining the Royal Navy he converted to the Protestant faith. As to what he drew out of it, that was anybody's guess.

Together they travelled to the Highlands. Whether it was the Good Book or whether Theo booked into a clinic for treatment for his mental state of mind, Tina wasn't quite sure, but it did the trick!

But before his trip, he caused havoc in Tina's life.

From the hotel, she didn't go out anywhere, as she buried herself in work, and had a very meagre wardrobe. Except on this particular Sunday; Gina had insisted that she go over to lunch, and see her mum again. As they were about to sit down to eat, the doorbell rang. Gina went to answer it and in rushed Theo, shouting, 'I know that she is here!'

Tina hid in the kitchen, as she didn't want any disturbance in someone else's home. But it was Gina's mum who stood up, as a true Italian, saying, 'You are no longer welcome here, so get out!'

In the past, they had often come to lunch, and to see baby Paul. Theo would show off with his culinary creations, and got on well with Mrs Santori, as she was able to converse with Theo in her own language.

32

Soon it was Christmas week, with everybody rushing about buying presents and decorations for a tree. But not Tina; she was busy moving house. She had found a position in Chelsea, in a residential club where she had a nice flat. It was a solid, turn of the century building with high ceilings and tall windows. The clientele were mainly businessmen, staying from Monday to Friday, spending weekends with their families.

Tina missed out on the festive season, settling in and starting in a new job. The flat next to hers was occupied by a young couple with a little girl. The wife was German, named Remy; the husband was Scottish, called Angus, and their offspring was called Renata.

They ran a bar, serving light snacks, as a franchise from the club. Tina soon got pally with Remy, and told her about Paul, and her visits to the nursery. She was making plans to get custody, and have Paul live with her. Remy got quite excited and suggested that they should hire a nanny and share the expenses. However, Theo had left instructions with Social Services that his wife was on drugs and an alcoholic and totally unfit to be a mother. Tina couldn't understand that a social worker wasn't prepared to come and see her and the home environment.

They took Theo's word as gospel and that was the end of the matter! This was such a low blow, and an attack on her character that she didn't know which way to turn. She had always been almost teetotal, apart from an occasional glass of

109

wine. And as for drugs, they were totally taboo; she wouldn't have known one substance from another.

Her old friend Stella was completely teetotal and the two of them got their highs from all the excitement of their comings and goings; in painting the town red! Theo had been a heavy drinker himself, when they first met, up to six vodkas in the course of an evening, although it didn't have any effect on him.

Tina pointed out that she didn't approve, that three drinks at the most should have been enough. But then he reported that back in the Middle East he would finish the whole bottle and that they used to have competitions with other captains 'to drink them under the table'. Hearing such news, Tina made it quite clear that if he needed that much alcohol there was no point in them meeting again. She hated a weak man, having seen evidence of such behaviour in her sister's husband.

Tina was pleasantly surprised to see that he was able to stop almost completely. From that time on, he stuck to two drinks. At home they didn't keep any, apart from sherry. He would have a small glass before his dinner. But not even wine, Tina wouldn't buy it, except for visitors.

She had been so sure of winning the custody, since she had placed Paul in the local authority care voluntarily and as a temporary measure, and had not been behind with her payments for his stay.

Remy was upset too, and never wanted to set eyes on such a man, who was cruel enough to use his own son as a pawn to his own evil ends.

Tina's predecessor at the club was Anna. She and her husband, and Anna's younger sister, had shared the flat, which was now Tina's. Anna was seven months pregnant, and had suffered from morning sickness, so her sister had come to stay, to cook the breakfast as she couldn't face anything fried.

110

They were all Polish nationals, although they had lived in London for some years. Anna was on the lookout for a secondhand cot and pram for her baby. This gave Tina an idea: since Paul's were in excellent condition, she would sell them. A little extra cash wouldn't go amiss.

Theo was still in London, due to fly out at the end of January. Tina rang his office, hoping to make arrangements to hire a van and collect her belongings. He sounded rather too cheerful in reporting that there had been a fire and all her stuff in the backroom was burnt or damaged. It sounded too flippant to believe. So Tina rang the office manager, Nigel, when Theo was out for lunch, and asked him, 'Has there been a fire in the storeroom?'

'No, whatever made you ask that?' he answered.

'Theo told me that all my things were ruined, when I made arrangements to collect my belongings.'

'The bastard, he sold the lot, including your clothes. And was happy to tell everyone that the woman was your size!' informed Nigel.

'What woman are you referring to?' Tina asked.

'He sold your stuff to a young Greek couple he hardly knew. They ran a fish and chip shop somewhere in Fulham. The wife was delighted with the designer labels!'

Nigel wasn't over-keen on Theo, although he and his wife were witnesses at their wedding, and came to the flat for drinks afterwards. He saw Theo as a reckless playboy rather than a serious businessman. Later Tina was to learn that his partner wanted him out for not pulling his weight. Most days he didn't even get to the office until ten a.m. and took two hours for lunch, and then left at five-thirty p.m. sharp.

It was his partner who had advised him to go back to the Middle East, and do what he was good at rather than loaf around the office.

Hearing the news of his heinous act on top of losing the custody application, Tina felt utterly defeated. All her quality outfits disposed of and sold. It would be a long time before she could wear anything like that again, if ever. Should she report the matter to the police, she wondered. But she decided against it, believing that the very evil force in the man gave him a winning hand. It was yet another case of turning the other cheek!

But she sank into pits of despair, and cried all night over the unfairness of it all. How could she carry on after this?

But in the morning light, duty called. She would put on a brave face against the world and try to find solace in her work and new friends. Had she given in, she would leave herself homeless and jobless. Tina had more backbone that that; she had survived against adversity so far and wasn't going to quit now!

33

She had a new-found friend in Rosa, who hailed from Switzerland, and worked as a nurse in South Kensington. She too had experienced an unhappy marriage with a chap from Egypt. However, she had turned the tables on a vindictive husband by paying a visit to his flat with a large pair of scissors. She had cut up his suits, and left his shoes soaking in bleach lined up in the bathtub! Tina liked her style, and wondered that perhaps there was hope yet. Rosa's motto in life was very positive: 'If at first you fail, then you try again!'

She persuaded Tina to go dancing again at the Café de Paris. The foxhound was no longer around, but then again he was never a dancing man; he had been there for a totally different reason. The manager, with a cute smile and friendly ways, had retired, but the place was still as popular as ever. On Saturday nights it was so full that the latecomers couldn't get in; exceeding the numbers would have breached the fire regulations.

Rosa was also a regular visitor to Tina's flat, and helped to lift her spirits. After three months at the flat, Tina received a letter from Theo with photographs enclosed of a snowbound villa, and one of his chauffeur brushing snow off the bonnet of a Merc. He wasn't in the Middle East after all, but in Austria, working for a subsidiary company of the oil industry that he had been with eighteen years.

He asked Tina to go over and live with him; she would like all that snow! If she agreed, he would send her the air tickets

113

whenever was convenient for her to travel. Tina didn't even reply. Reading between the lines, she figured that what he and his chauffeur lacked was a cook/housekeeper. And, indeed, they found one; a nineteen-year-old German girl called Helle.

Within two years, there were five of them! The firstborn boy was fathered by Theo, and the second boy was by the chauffeur! He was now connected with a business of overland container lorries from Iran to Europe. A convoy of forty trucks, escorted by security guards, would travel through the bandit country. The route passed through Afghanistan and eastern Turkey. Tina received photos of two of these large containers being ambushed; tyres shot, and rolling over into a ravine. Tina's thoughts formed a wicked streak, that perhaps the bandits might blight Theo's schemes as well.

Tina was relatively contented workwise at the club, but after a while she began to wonder if she would earn a lot more working in a hotel, although she couldn't expect the same type of accommodation.

But, since she had to accept the fact that Paul wasn't going to live with her, she might as well concentrate on earning more towards a new wardrobe and holidays. She also started divorce proceedings, citing mental cruelty.

While Theo was abroad, he had asked Jeremy to visit Paul on his behalf. One Sunday afternoon Tina met him at the nursery, and the three of them went to a park for ice creams. Jeremy casually dropped a hint that Theo was going back to the Persian Gulf, and was making arrangements to take Paul to live with him. Tina asked him whether Theo would be coming over himself.

Jeremy's answer chilled her to the bone. He replied that some of his cronies would call to pick him up. Although she didn't show any alarm, before leaving the nursery she asked the matron to keep a close eye on her son, but didn't elaborate. Soon after, one of the house-mothers rang Tina to say that there were two Arabic-looking men parked outside the gates in a large station-wagon, asking the children, 'Which one of you is Paul?'

When asked why they wanted to know, they had simply said, 'We are friends of his dad and wanted to say hello!'

Tina asked the caller to keep Paul safely indoors until she got there. To prevent his kidnapping, Tina made him a ward of court.

Theo's ploy was to get back at Tina for not following him to Austria. So Tina obtained legal aid for her divorce battle, and applied for alimony and maintenance. Both were turned down! The case didn't come up until 1977, when she was an executive housekeeper in a very large hotel in West London. She received a copy of Theo's sworn statement regarding his income and means. His salary was quoted as £37,000 a year, tax free, plus a free company house with servants. Tina had to appear in the High Court family division twice. Firstly in regard to maintenance payments to support Paul and secondly in private chambers, with a dire and unexpected outcome. Tina was told that because she was living apart from her son she wasn't entitled to any maintenance. As for the alimony, again the four men were in agreement that since her husband was domiciled abroad he didn't have to pay her a penny!

Tina pointed out his very substantial income, and that her own in comparison was a minute percentage of his salary. But Theo's solicitor, the man that she had often met when they lived in Kensington, had the cheek to announce that Tina's own salary was above average and she got her food as well!

No doubt he was paid a nice backhander to act as an adversary.

They all seemed so smug, their handiwork achieved. Tina gave them a long stare, but there was no point in shouting and being unladylike. She concluded to blunt their joy by saying, 'That being the case, I will stay married!'

To Theo's solicitor she said, 'Do inform your good man that you have failed; now it's up to him to divorce me instead!'

34

She had never had any difficulty in finding work, and whenever she went for an interview she was normally hired on the spot. She applied to be a housekeeper, which she enjoyed the most; no more waitressing for her, nor late hours. She would work office hours, live in and take all her meals in the hotel restaurant. It felt such a luxury, having long afternoons and evenings to herself. And there were set annual holidays and sick pay as well. She didn't even need any time for food shopping or cooking. It really was a novelty, compared to her previous jobs, when she had been on the go for sixteen hours a day.

The hotel was privately owned and situated in Bloomsbury. The manager was called Arthur Lawrence, and he was a retired bank manager. He informed Tina that he didn't know much about housekeeping operations, so she was expected to do her own thing. She was pleased and regarded it as a challenge.

The chambermaids were Spanish and Portuguese; very reliable and hard-working. The porters and restaurant staff were all Irish, and pleasantly lively. Most of the staff were living in, and had their quarters in the basement. Tina, the head chef and the assistant manageress had rooms on the floors with the hotel guests.

The assistant manageress was a very attractive divorcee, and professional in her work, but at the end of a day she would sit in the bar and catch the eye of some goodlooking businessman and end up in the same bed! When this became too obvious, as it didn't reflect well on the image of the hotel, Mrs Duncan was banished to a staff house nearby to share with reception staff.

One of the house porters, Peter, was very young, not quite seventeen yet, and had such a sweet baby-face. One night he had experimented with beer, with a mishap to follow. He came to Tina shamefaced, asking for clean sheets, because his bed was wet!

Tina went along with him to check his room and see just how wet was his mattress. She was clucking like a mother hen that he was long past bedwetting age. The mattress was soaked through, and had to be thrown out as it would have been a health hazard. He looked rather scared by then. Tina was always fairminded, but if she wanted something done then that would be so. It was Peter's day off work, and Tina observed that he had used stickytape to put up some horrid posters, thus damaging the paintwork. She decided to teach him a lesson, to keep off the booze and be tidy. She ripped the posters down, and ordered him to redecorate his room that day. In the maintenance shop they found some paint, a roller, brushes and dustsheets. All the blankets and bedding were bundled up to go to a laundry room. Tina asked Peter to make a start, and keep at it. When he was done, only then would he get a dry mattress and clean bedding.

Tina was just coming out of the restaurant after having her dinner when Peter asked her to inspect his work. He had done a good job of it, and appeared rather pleased with his handiwork. He was as good as gold after that, but moved on before Tina. It was some six years later when they bumped into each other in the Café de Paris. He had really filled out into a man, and was now an army soldier! He asked Tina to do a Viennese waltz with him, and was rather nimble-footed. When the dance ended, he said, 'By the way, since that paint job, I have been right off my lager!'

'I am mighty pleased to hear that something good came out of that palaver!' was Tina's comment.

The proprietor of the hotel was a charming man in his late sixties, and lived in West Sussex. He came over for a visit every fortnight with his chauffeur, who doubled as a gardener. He would carry in a laundry hamper and fill it with clean linen and towels. He would replenish and tidy up the windowboxes with whatever blooms Tina requested, and they really looked attractive against the white walls of the building. When Mr Burton got to know Tina better he would accompany her to check around the house, rather than take tea in the lounge. From then on, when leaving, he would shake Tina's hand, enclosing a neatly-folded £10 note into her palm. This was their secret; and a very nice one too!

When the autumn came, Mr Burton had a request for Tina. His grandson was coming to London to work as a trainee in a merchant bank in the city. As James was rather shy, and hadn't been away from home, could Tina mother him a bit, until he got used to living on his own?

Tina was delighted, and fixed him up with a nice room on the top floor. She found a solid desk in a storeroom and got her linen-keeper to run up some large cushions to make the room more homely than a standard one.

James soon got into the swing of London life, except he wasn't terribly keen shopping on his own. Together they went to get him some trendy shirts and a couple of cashmere sweaters. They would often have dinner together, and Tina asked the nightporters to take him a pot of coffee at the appointed hour, so that he would be up in time to have a full breakfast before setting off to the bank.

He found a girlfriend at work, a real 'sloane ranger', and Tina left him alone! On Mr Burton's next visit she informed him that his grandson was now a fully-fledged man, and the old boy was well pleased.

Two girls who worked in reception became her new close

friends. Anne was English and Bridget was French. They went dancing or to a cinema twice a week, but never as a threesome. Since Anne was Bridget's line manager, it never paid to fraternise.

Tina had met an elderly chap who had been born in Iceland, but had lived in Canada for some thirty years until his wife died. He was always dressed up in a dickybow, as he frequented London casinos. He was a member of three of them, and asked Tina to accompany him. She wanted to see inside, but didn't understand gambling, nor was she interested, except to watch.

He was the type of man who appeared to be very prosperous, but he was not academic, and an utter bore! Therefore, Tina invited Bridget along to make it more interesting. Soon Alun got fed up having her tacking along everywhere. Tina told him straight: 'Where I go, Bridget goes too; it's either two of us, or neither!'

They had some good times, but Tina wouldn't have gone anywhere alone with Alun.

With Anne, she would go shopping or have a picnic in a park. Tina was now able to visit Paul during the week as well, as she could get to the nursery before teatime. At weekends, she was able to take him to the zoo, or to a play area in the park.

35

Tina managed a long-awaited holiday during the summer, when Paul went to a seaside camp with a group of children, and their house-mothers. No more sailing, this time she flew out of Heathrow to Helsinki. From there she travelled by train to her sister's apartment in Turku.

Irene had arranged her holidays to coincide with Tina's and they went by coach the eighty kilometres to the farm.

Mama was brown as a berry, from working so much outdoors. It was very hot, the temperature was 30–35°C every day. Tina slept in a dressing room of the sauna. It was a little cooler there, and often used by visitors staying overnight.

It felt so good, getting her fingers into soft soil, weeding in the kitchen garden. The scent of flowers and white roses on both sides of the porch filled the air. It was like being in another world, no sound of traffic, only farm animals bleating or mooing and cats and dogs making their familiar sounds!

Brother Leo didn't care for cars, he was a motorbike fanatic. He always had the biggest one on the market. It was handy for taking shortcuts along footpaths and country lanes. Tina went pillion riding to visit neighbours, as was expected of her.

Tina enjoyed mama's cooking, and strawberries from the garden every day. There was a fair amount of entertaining, with visitors coming from near and far. But all too soon she had to depart, as duty called in London.

She really enjoyed her work at the hotel, having organised

the department herself. But as a saying goes, 'All good things come to an end!' There were to be major changes to come. The manager, Mr Lawrence, was to retire, for the second time, to his cottage in Cornwall. Mrs Duncan moved on to become a hotel inspector. Her replacement was a young man who went by the book, as if still at a class at catering college – there was no leeway in his reckoning! The new manager was from South Africa, although born in Dublin, and a real calamity!

In tow was her twenty-two-year-old daughter, who replaced Bridget in reception. Her husband had been a minister, and they had travelled as missionaries until he died. She treated staff as if they were slaves.

One morning Tina heard her shouting in the staff canteen, and went to see what it was all about. She was calling her hard-working chambermaids 'greedy pigs' for eating all the profits! She was actually poking their plates with a fork, demonstrating that two rashers of bacon and two eggs was criminal! From now on it would be cut down to one each, and if they dared to complain they would get nothing but porridge!

The maids looked to Tina to stand up for them, which is exactly what she did. Although Mrs Moore was her immediate boss, she also knew for certain that Mr Burton wouldn't tolerate such conduct. She herself didn't hold with such a Victorian attitude and told her so.

'Mrs Moore, you have overstepped the mark. In your office, please, I have more to say on the subject!'

Once the door was closed, she started on her defence.

'My main aim is to increase profits, and I don't give a damn how I do it!'

Tina replied, 'You are no longer roaming in the African bush, you have landed yourself in the cosmopolitan city of London. Things are different here! The maids do heavy physical work and need good meals. Let's face it, you wouldn't be able to drive your car unless you filled up the tank now and then. Horsepower or manpower is all the same; we are talking about energy here! Should you harass or insult my staff again, I will join the exodus, and take off without further notice!'

Tina very seldom lost her temper, but when it happened everyone was on their toes. She had a one-track mind, and wasn't going to let the woman off the hook until she mended her ways.

After her taking over, the staff were very subdued, creeping about like ghosts. Their previous happy chatter and laughter had died.

Tina had another encounter with Mrs Moore, saying: 'If you carry on like this, you will be out of the job yourself; so think on that before starting on another rampage!'

There was a head housekeeper's position going in nearby Holborn. Tina went along to see the general manager and told him about the problems up the road. Mr Fellowes listened to her tale of woe and asked, 'How soon can you start, tomorrow or next week?'

It was obvious that Mrs Moore wasn't going to change, so Tina left her to it. The very next day she was at her desk across the square. This was Friday morning. On Monday morning, before nine o'clock, Mrs Moore was on the line, asking her to come back, to stop everyone walking out on her!

'You had it coming, and I am too busy to hear about it right now!' was Tina's comment.

At twelve-thirty Mrs Moore was on the phone again, asking Tina to go over to have lunch with her. She declined the invitation but listened this time, to hear what the staffing situation was. She promised to send her new staff over on their day off work. And to encourage them, they would have to be paid daily, cash in hand. She appeared to be satisfied for the time being.

That same day at the close of working hours, a kitchen porter came to tell Tina that there was a group of women at the back door asking for her. These were some of her former chambermaids, who had worked in the hotel, some for six years, and had been loyal to her throughout. they were getting on a bit as well; Maria, the eldest, was nearing fifty. She spoke for the others.

'Please, madam, we want to be with you.'

Tina felt as if she had deserted a sinking ship, and invited them to her office. She explained that as much as she wanted to do so, at the present time she had a full staff. Maybe at a later date, if any vacancies came up. Meanwhile, they should gang together, to do their work and make the most of it. The three younger ones couldn't stand it, and would leave anyway. The older girls, including Maria, took her advice, and stayed another couple of months, until Tina was in the position to employ them.

Mrs Moore was happy with her relief staff, but it wasn't enough. Could she not keep some of them permanently? She was willing to pay them higher wages. Tina's answer was adamant: absolutely not, except maybe one of the housekeepers.

Rita was very conscientious, but too much of an old-timer. Although she was Tina's assistant, she decided that Rita was surplus to requirements and planned to train one of the floor housekeepers for the post.

When she asked Rita whether she wouldn't rather be top dog and take over Tina's old job, she moved on happily. But sadly, she couldn't cope unless she had a full staff and no hassles!

Mrs Moore kept ringing, as if Tina was still with the same company. To sort out 'the cockup' once and for all and for the sake of Mr Burton, she made it clear to Mrs Moore that she didn't owe any favours to her personally! She suggested that she put an advert in *The Evening Standard*, but give Tina's present office number. Since she knew the terms and conditions, she interviewed a number of applicants. The ones that she found suitable, she sent across to confirm about starting work.

This was her second week in the new job, and she was already up to no good! Mr Fellowes stepped into her office asking, 'Why are you interviewing people when we have a full staff?'

Tina invited him to take a seat, so she could tell him all about it. He was annoyed with himself, having missed all the moonlighting that had been going on. However, he found the whole caper rather innovative in helping 'thy neighbour'. Tina explained that she didn't want to lose her good name by walking out, so was making amends with unfinished business. He sympathised with her reasoning, but on departing made the remark, 'As long as you don't start an employment agency as a little sideline!'

Mr Burton had missed one visit, as he had been on a Caribbean cruise. On his return, James had informed him about all the changes that had taken place recently. When he next visited, he could feel an atmosphere in the hotel; things were clearly not right. Even some regular guests had cancelled their bookings, and staffwise he saw too many new faces. Mrs Moore had been in the job just over a month when Mr Burton sacked her 'on the spot' and the daughter was to go too! The old boy stayed on the whole week trying to restore the business. It really is incredible how much damage can be caused by having the wrong person in charge.

Tina kept in touch with Anne for some two years after leaving, and heard all the news about what 'the rivals' were up to. In her new job she hadn't fraternised with the staff, although she was very fond of Angela, the head receptionist, and they usually had their meals together.

36

In that particular hotel there were four trainees at any given time, doing their practical before taking their finals at catering college. They had to do three months in each department, and it was up to the departmental head to send a monthly report to their college tutors.

Tina had one young man from Wales who had already done food and beverage in the bar and restaurant and hadn't fared at all well, getting his tariffs and measures all cock-eyed! Tina was hoping that he might fare better in housekeeping and maintenance, but sadly it was not to be. To start with, his hair was too long, falling over his eyes. Tina asked him to go to the barbers and said that she would see him in the morning with a short back and sides.

The next morning there was no change. As the rest of the housekeeping staff were female, apart from porters and linen-keepers, Tina decided that if he wanted to be one of the girls then she would pretty him up some!

In a sewing kit she found a red ribbon, and with a great fuss she made him a nice ponytail. That very day, he went for a haircut.

Then there was a problem in waking up in the mornings. Many times Tina had to send one of the porters to tilt his bed to get him out of it! She did it once herself, tipping him to the floor and asking, 'Cliff, am I right in thinking that you are awake now?'

Tina's reports on his work (an eye for detail, aptitude, timekeeping, conduct in teamwork, own initiative) were all rotten, but the absolute truth.

He niggled her. She didn't understand why was he so disinterested, when apart from that, he had a quick mind and a sense of humour. One day Tina asked him to stay behind and have a private chat. She learned that his parents were hoteliers, and he had been pushed into the same trade, which he didn't want to and was trying to find ways to drop out. He wanted to be an accountant. Tina wished him luck, whichever it was going to be.

Ten years later, when Tina bought a flat in Chiswick, and joined the residents' committee, who should walk into a meeting but Cliff, wearing a Burberry coat. She was pleased to note that he had done well as an accountant, having bought his own place, as there were no rented flats in the block.

They had a lovely staff party before Christmas. Mr Fellowes suggested that they should dress up, as in going to a ball! He was in a bottle-green velvet dinner jacket; the junior managers had the same getup but in maroon velvet, and dickybows!

Tina herself had a long black evening dress, and a red rose pinned to her lapel. They served the junior staff as 'mine hosts'. It was a party to be remembered fondly.

After working there for just over a year, Tina hurt her back. The linen-porter was off sick, the laundry van was running late due to a driver being off sick as well, so she decided to help, with dire results. She lifted a very heavy hamper, and slipped on a recently-mopped floor. She slipped a disc on both sides of her lower back. An ambulance came, Tina was given a shot of morphine to kill the pain, and strapped into a stretcher. She was in a hospital in Fulham for five weeks, unable to get out of bed, nor walk. She was in a great deal of pain, and needed bedrest. Every day she had two visitors from the hotel, who took it in turns so as not to exceed the numbers. The head receptionist, Angela, even brought her weekly wage packets over, which were piling up in the ward sister's safe.

Yes, in those days all the staff were paid weekly in cash; monthly salaries paid to the bank account didn't come about until the mid-Eighties as a norm for senior staff.

Tina was confined to a hospital bed in a very large ward, the size of a warehouse, with beds on both sides facing each other. On her left was a lady over eighty and on her right was a woman in her thirties. She was wired up to tubes and drips.

Tina didn't swallow her sleeping pills, but hid them all in a bedside drawer. In the small hours of one night, from the next bed, there came a ear-piercing shriek. 'I have nothing to life for, so why are you trying to keep me alive?' She ripped the drips and tubes like a wild creature.

A night nurse came running, calling doctors to an emergency. But it was too late, she died before her eyes.

The next night the old lady on Tina's other side gave up the fight too, but went without causing such a racket!

That afternoon Mr Fellowes himself came to visit, and Tina told him that it might be her turn next. He had a word with the hospital administration, so that she could be moved to a smaller unit which was less distressing, as he was anxious to have her back at work. So it came to pass that Tina was wheeled to a private wing, with only three other patients. All had fractured or broken their hips in a fall.

Tina was given a lumbar puncture into her upper spine, to see whether the discs were knitting together. The houseman told her that she needed an operation to have a metal clip inserted to her lower back on both sides, to hold them together. Tina asked for a second pinion, but the specialist had come to the same conclusion. But Tina decided not to have anything metal in her bones; it might be worse, and if she was to be left in a wheelchair then she would do so without the operation.

The lumbar puncture itself is not a pleasant experience. Tina felt as if her brains were being drained. She was warned of severe headaches to follow. By this time she was able to walk to the loo, and there she blacked out. Her two visitors had been sitting by her empty bed for some time, fearing the worst, until the nurse went to investigate her whereabouts.

Towards the end of her stay, the consultant was very pleased to say that Tina had made the right decision in refusing the operation. Being a former athlete, she had strong bones, and the discs had healed nicely. She needed physiotherapy for quite a while yet, but could go back to work.

In the mornings she had great difficulty in getting out of bed, as she felt very stiff, like in being in a straitjacket. But she wouldn't give in, and got up two hours before going to her office downstairs, to do exercises to warm up and get flexible. Apart from this, she coped quite well on strong painkillers, and didn't take any more time off work.

In the next six months she had to deal with two situations that she could have done without. She had a maintenance man who was fairly competent in his work, but rather a rough diamond. He was a real East-End lad, and keen at amateur boxing. He had a young family with two children and often talked about how hard it was making ends meet.

As in most hotels, guests forget items in the bedrooms when they depart. Housekeepers would bring them to Tina's office, label them with the date and room number, and enter the same into the 'lost and found' books. Items were kept in the storeroom for six months, and some were claimed or posted on. But a lot was disposed of when the six months had expired. Good quality clothing, Tina would share among the staff, but this time she had some children's clothing: jumpers, jackets, shoes and pyjamas. She decided to give them to Tom, to take to his children.

Soon after this, on doing an inventory in his workshop-cum-storeroom, she noticed a number of light fittings and boxes of bulbs missing. She suspected Tom of stealing them, since he had the keys all day. Tina confronted him with her discovery. He admitted selling them to his mate, who was an electrician.

Tina sacked him, but he regarded it 'as a storm in a teacup', and not worth a fortune. However, theft small or large is really the same thing in a hotel, when a workman can no longer be trusted with keys to hotel bedrooms.

Tom was shaking his fists over Tina's desk, threatening 'to give her a good hiding'. She stood her ground, even though there was only the two of them in the office. Luckily, he came to his senses, dropped his raised fists, handed his keys over, and left.

At the end of the day, Mr Fellowes was in agreement with her actions, but they decided not to take court action. He wouldn't get a reference, and might regret his stealing.

But the next day, he arrived with the two children and his wife to see Tina. His wife was a real trooper, and brought Tom along to apologise and shake Tina's hand. The young wife also thanked her for the children's clothes, for which she would be eternally grateful.

Later on, Tina had a vacancy for a live-in chambermaid, and informed an employment agency which the hotel used. A young girl turned up wearing a heavy overcoat, as it was winter. She had some experience and was keen to start, and her references checked out. But when she put on a work uniform, she couldn't hide her condition. Tina felt rather let down, and rang the agency. Why had they sent a girl who was over four months pregnant? The heavy coat had fooled the man at the agency as well.

Tina took Leslie aside to ask why she had been so deceitful; couldn't she go home to her family? It turned out that she was in dire straits. Brought up in a home as an orphan, the father of her unborn child had scarpered as soon as he found out. So Tina decided to stand by by her. The girl had a nice room, good food and should save as much as possible and mix with other girls, but keep away from pubs. When she was seven months or so on her time, Tina promised to arrange a social worker to get her into a mother and baby hostel. As long as she did her work and gave no trouble, she had nothing to worry about.

The other girls were very supportive, but some of the young porters were hoping to 'go cherry picking', because she was already in the family way! When this got to Tina's ears, the porters had a good reason to run for cover!

Mr Fellowes found himself a wife from the hotel staff. He was longing to settle somewhere more quiet, and found a manager's post in the country, near a golf course, which was a bonus.

Tina began to get restless herself, she was not hankering for country life. All she wanted was self-contained accommodation, with her own kitchen, to be able to entertain a few of her friends.

Working and living in a hotel is okay when you are young and are more likely to go out in the evenings, but when you are past that stage it feels very transient, and lacking in home comforts.

37

Tina found herself a position as a manageress of a self-catering hostel in Earl's Court, with a beautiful walled-in back garden which overlooked a sprinkler fountain on the patio of the hotel next door. But before her flat was to be vacated, she had a week's break after giving in her notice at the hotel.

Theo was on vacation in London for two months. They had met at the nursery as they had to make arrangements regarding Paul's future.

On arrival Theo had stayed at The Gloucester Hotel in Harrington Gardens, but for such a long stay found it too costly, preferring something self-contained, as he enjoyed cooking. And of all things, Tina was surprised at his gall to go back to the house in Harrington Gardens, where they had lived as a family. Of course, he didn't have to deal with Mr Collier, as there was a Spanish couple in the housekeeper's flat to do the lettings and collect rents. Tina had, prior to meeting him, arranged an appointment with the Social Services department, hoping to find foster parents for Paul in the area. As he had already started in a primary school, living with a large crowd of children, constantly changing wasn't settled nor an ideal situation – far from it. Social Services had advertised and got two offers: one family was in Oxford, and the other in Middlesex. Tina opted for the latter, as the family had another foster boy who was some two years older.

Tina prayed that they would get on, and be company for each other. Surprisingly, Theo went along with this, as his approval was required, since they had a joint custody. Tina felt that a week's break really wasn't enough to travel home, so he suggested that she use his flatlet, to have a rest, and be only walking distance from her new job at the hostel. She had accumulated a fair amount of luggage, so took up the offer rather than book into a guesthouse.

She was to be there alone, as Theo had to make a trip to Barcelona to open a branch office for the oil company. He would leave his keys with the housekeeper.

When Tina got out of the taxi there was Theo outside the house! Her heart fell, wondering what kind of a trick he had pulled this time. His story was that he had had his briefcase stolen, and had to wait for a new passport.

All the flatlets were furnished with two single beds, although most were let as a single occupancy. They had a metal base, one being collapsible, to slip under the other during the day, to allow more living space. Had it meant sharing a bed with Theo, she would have called another taxi and made alternative arrangements.

Tina had only stayed three days when she had a surprise visitor. Theo had gone to his old office in the city, and the person visiting had rung the housekeeper's bell. She called Tina on the internal phone to say that there was a girl at the door, looking for her husband; would she like to deal with it?

There stood a girl in her twenties, and a minicab full of suitcases. Her first words were a revelation: 'Oh, my God, you *are* his wife, I have seen the photo album!'

Tina asked, 'Who are you?'

'I am Helle, we lived together in Austria. And I have come over to marry him, my two children are with my sister in Peckham.'

Tina told Helle that unfortunately there wasn't enough room for three of them, and advised her to go the nearest hotel, the one where Tina had done all that waitressing, so that she could dismiss the minicab.

133

'But I have no money to pay for the hotel!' Helle wailed.

'Don't worry about it, I will ring Theo at the office, and ask him to come over to see you, and sort out the payment!'

That evening he was so flustered that he didn't know which way to turn. Tina was delighted that his scam had backfired. He had moved Helle to a bed and breakfast hotel, not being prepared to spend more than an absolute minimum.

The next day, his passport materialised, and he was happy to get away to Spain! Tina herself had a sneaky feeling that Helle would be 'a bad loser'. She was only twenty-one, but appeared hard and bitter, and very tartily dressed. Lots of make-up, and too low-cut a dress for daytime wear.

Tina enjoyed her break. She sunbathed on the roof or in a nearby park, and went shopping.

Theo returned when she was ready to move to the hostel. He even helped and did some minor electrical work, so that Tina would have proper lighting. This was on Saturday. He was to return to the Persian Gulf the following Monday. But just as Tina had suspected, on that Sunday he got 'some of his own medicine'! Helle's mother had flown over to demand money for a breach of promise to marry her daughter, and maintenance to feed the children. She had physically gone for his throat, and all four of them would stay until he paid the money expected. The police had been called to restrain the two women, who had 'gone wild'! Tina never found out whether they got any maintenance, but thought it very unlikely. It would have been like getting blood out of a stone.

Helle's mother had gone home and the boys stayed in Peckham. As for Helle, she began working as a hostess in a West End nightclub; Tina had put the right label on her!

Theo's original scam was to persuade Tina once again to fly with him to Iran, now that she was in between jobs. If she refused, then he would prolong the divorce hearing, as they had cohabited, living in the same flat for a few days. Of course, he had expected to share the bed as well, but it was a vain hope! Helle was very willing to take him on permanently, but he had lost interest long since, as it would have meant supporting a family. That's when he told Tina that only one of the boys was his anyway. But he was happy enough to fly away, with only a few scratches, as he had found another twenty-year-old girl in Barcelona who was to go with him as his mistress. Thus he was trying to make Tina jealous, but it didn't work; after all the let-downs, all her feelings had died. So she approved wholeheartedly that it was a very good arrangement, having one woman, rather than a number. He was such a playboy, he could charm the birds off the trees, until they saw his 'true colours'.

38

The hostel was part of a group of four near to one another. They were privately owned by a wealthy Polish lady who had a beautiful house in 'The Boltons'. She lived there with her second husband, a toyboy.

Tina would earn less than in the hotel, having a free flat to go with the job. But this time she got around that, not losing out financially. She would run it single-handed, and not pay an assistant; only wages for a part-time cleaner. This meant that she had very long hours, seven days a week, but she had done that before.

It was an all-female hostel, with only forty-five beds. She selected her residents well, hoping to run an orderly but happy house. She had plenty of time to do her shopping, while the cleaner was on the premises. and in no time at all, some of the girls started to suggest that she must go out dancing occasionally, and offered to house-sit, should there be a fire or some other emergency.

One of the residents, who was a very striking, Elizabeth Taylor lookalike, Colombian girl, wanted Tina to go with her. This time, for a change, it was The Hammersmith Palais every Friday night. Ken McIntosh and his big band had taken residence there from The Empire in Leicester Square.

Her new employer, Mrs Orfinski, came to visit when Tina had worked there for two weeks. She was so pleased, that she said, 'This is "your castle". From now on I shan't interfere unless you need me to.'

Tina felt great, having such a free hand. However, this

time she didn't bank the monies, but took it all in a plastic carrier over to the Boltons weekly. Together with Mrs Orfinski, they would go over the books and balance sheets, while enjoying a pot of tea with her freshly-baked cake.

Her husband popped over once a month, to bring her cleaning supplies.

Another stray cat appeared. It jumped down from the garden wall when Tina was sunbathing. He was trying to make friends, and after a first saucer of milk decided to take root! Tina named him 'Burlington Berti', because he looked so dressed up, with a black coat, white shirt-front and popsocks! Berti was to be a great comfort to her.

Summer 1976 remains one of the hottest recorded, and the only summer Tina had experienced with water being rationed. Twice a day for a few hours the taps were dry. Even in her garden there appeared large cracks on the ground, and the grass had long since burned to brown. And green leaves in a large tree dropped down, their textures that of latex!

39

Since their Sunday outing to visit cousin Nicholas, Tina had known about a legacy – this time in Theo's family. The two men had discussed it in front of Auntie Betty.

Theo's grandfather had been a high-ranking officer during the revolution between Greece and Turkey. While he was there, he acquired a large plot of land by the Black Sea. He willed it to his children, Betty, Alec and Albert, who was Theo's father, to be passed on to their issue.

At that time, the property had been divided into twenty-three equal plots, and only three had been sold. A mosque had been built on one, and hunting lodges on another two, to be used by parties to go shooting wild boar.

The total land was half a square mile.

As Theo's father had died of a heart attack, his share was now equally divided between Theo and sister Glenda. Uncle Alec was an executor of the legacy, and Tina received all this information from him over the phone, confirmed by cousin Nicholas, who by this time had inherited his mother Betty's share. He also divulged the details of the name of the property and that the land-registry was in the town of Ismai.

During that few days with Theo, she had brought the subject up, to ask whether he had been able to get his money out, as far as the others appeared to have encountered difficulties. Tina was hoping to be reimbursed for some of her expenses while keeping the family together. Theo was earning a high salary, which allowing for inflation, by today's scale would have been over £200,000 a year. That is when he suggested that if she was lucky enough to get his share out, she could keep it, and he advised her to contact Uncle Alec.

During this hot summer in July, Tina made arrangements to fly out to Paris for a long weekend, and meet Alec there to get some legal documents. Two of her girls, both schoolteachers, were happy to hold the forts, and stay in Tina's flat rather than their basement room, which they shared.

On arrival at her hotel in France, Tina was to contact Alec. However, he had to fly out to Nice to see a dying friend. He urged Tina to go with him and stay a week, promising to cover her expenses. But as it was, Tina hadn't come prepared for another flight. Sadly, she didn't carry credit cards in those days, so she never got to meet Alec, as due to her work commitments she had to return to London. She didn't even explain to him that her very livelihood and roof over her head depended on keeping her job. A man with millions couldn't begin to understand her situation.

She made light of it not being so urgent. Perhaps they could get together during his next holiday in London.

On her return she went to visit cousin Nicholas, to learn more about her chances. She learned that Turkish law doesn't follow the international ruling, and furthermore, in Islam, women cannot own property nor other chattels. According to the Koran, they are without soul and equal to dogs! Therefore, Tina's plan was a non-starter, and Theo knew it. No doubt he enjoyed his little game.

Some years later Tina heard from cousin Nicholas that Theo had in fact got his money out, having so many contacts in Armenia, Iran and Turkey. But somebody, or maybe more than one person, was on the fiddle as there were ten bank accounts under names of people who didn't exist!

Nicholas himself had gone there to snoop around and take some photographs, and was arrested as an industrial spy and thrown into a Turkish jail. He was left there for three days, until rescued by the British embassy.

Some American corporations had made offers to buy some of the land to build a holiday resort, as it was a prime location, on a seafront, and with woodland as a backdrop. Still, this was one legacy that Tina couldn't claim rightfully hers; let the others fight over it, and may the best man win!

Tina was leading a quiet personal life, although around her it was lively, with so many young girls flitting about. The hot weather continued. Tina had put aside one evening a week when she expected to get all the rents in her sitting room, where she had her desk. The time allocated was between five and seven p.m. The residents would form a little queue at the doorway. On this particular evening, when the temperature was still very high, Vicky ran in to join the others, topless, tits flying, skimpy bikini bottoms and a chequebook in hand! The others didn't regard this as out of place, but Tina saw it as a bit over the top. She played a matronly warden, saying light-heartedly: 'Remember girls, knees together, and tits covered at all times!'

But since Vicky had seen Tina topless in her garden, from her window over the weekend, she was excused for doing likewise!

Anyway, such extreme heat made everyone want to strip off.

Vicky worked as a bank cashier, but in her free time she was a high-spirited prankster. Men were not allowed on the premises at all, as there was no communal lounge. It would have been very disruptive and unfair to a room-mate if the other entertained a boyfriend in the same bedroom.

Tina had a large notice printed for the hall, for everyone to be reminded of the rules of the house. In any case, there was enough coffee-bars and pubs open late in Earl's Court.

However, one middle-aged policeman had taken a fancy to a very pretty student from Egypt. This particular girl had confided to Tina that she was frightened of him. Because he was a policeman, he had told the poor girl that if she didn't go to bed with him he would have her deported as she had some problems with her visa. Tina was prepared when that man called at the door, off duty, and in civilian gear. He was trying to pull rank, to go to this girl's room, but Tina refused him entry!

Soon after, a much younger man rang the doorbell, saying that he was from CID, but he had no ID card, so Tina sent him packing too!

As it turned out, the poor man was quite genuine. Tina decided to pen down a little ditty about their second encounter, as follows:

Gentleman Caller

There at the door,
a smartly-dressed man,
'A call from the CID.'
'Fine, let's see some ID.'

Searching in every pocket,
empty-handed, found nothing.
'See that notice on the Wall?
MEN NOT ALLOWED IN THE HALL.'
Still insisting: 'I am a cop.'
'Mister, whoever you are,
it's time to hop.'

Very soon he is back at the door;
this time wearing a uniform.
'Oh, that was quick.'
'They are laughing at me,
in the local nick.
Now I am in real lumber.'
'Come on in, so I can take your number!'

'For so much trouble;
the nature of your call?'
'Oh, Home Office matter,
a passport fraud.'
'Mine is in order,
so that's all right!'
'It's one of your tenants,
I hope to find.'

'Lady, you are a dragon;
and a pain in the neck,
but wouldn't say no to a cuppa,
so, what the heck!'

'Coffee is perking,
take a pew;
so you can tell me,
a fib or two!'

Time went by detecting crime,
'Goodbye, mister, call anytime.
For law and order; I am on your side!'
This tall story is a true tale;
The boys in blue,
'What can I say?'

40

Tina had quite settled in with her cat and the garden. She continued to visit Mrs Orfinski weekly. Over their tea, she would give her a thoughtful look, and say: 'How I wish that you were my daughter!'

Tina was pleased with such a compliment, and yet quietly hoped that surely she wouldn't start any plans for adoption!

Tina went to the Café de Paris very seldom, as she was so tied to her work, not leaving the house unmanned. However, this particular Friday evening she had gone and 'dear Melvyn' was there! But he always left well before midnight; although divorced for many years, he was living with his daughters, and didn't want to worry them. They spent the evening together and he invited Tina to spend the weekend on his boat which he kept moored at Frinton-on-Sea, Essex. Tina was very tempted, but decided to keep their friendship platonic, and used work as an excuse.

After two years managing the hostel, Mrs Orfinski told Tina about her plans to sell out, and emigrate to Australia! She was longing for a warmer climate, to spend her retirement. After liquidating her assets, especially her house in Bolton Gardens she could live in luxury anywhere in the world. As their parting gift, she asked Tina to write her a poem, which she would frame, and gave her an antique brooch.

So, once again, Tina was like a gypsy on the move. She decided to get away from London for a while, to pastures new, and went to Eastbourne. She was longing for sun, sand

and sea, to have it all just for a summer season, for a period of six months. She found the position through an agency there, and once again worked in a hotel, which was a live-in post. The hotel was privately owned, with lots of family members in residence and overseeing the management. There was an American lady, a guest, who was teaching tennis players at the nearby courts during the season and spent the winter months at her house in Florida. She latched onto Tina. Whenever she went out, Mrs Marks was posted in the lounge by the front door, to follow her. Although she was a woman over sixty, they got on well, roaming the seafront and the entertainments on the pier. Bookings were mainly coach parties of retired folk, who would come for a week's stay.

One night there was an old lady knocking on Tina's door, saying, 'My friend Peggy is stiff!'

Tina, being fogged by sleep, asked her, 'Do you mean "stiff" as in being dead?'

'Oh, yes, yes, very dead, come with me!'

She had woken just about everyone in her party by then, which was after midnight. They were all in their night attire walking the corridors. She had been at the reception desk, but a youngish nightporter had told the poor soul to find Tina on the top floor. The old dears, some over seventy, had been on an outing, followed by a tea dance at the pier, and the excitement of the day had proved too much for Peggy.

She had her false teeth in a glass tumbler by her bedside, and looked peaceful, as if in preparation to go to her maker. Her room-mate, Edna, had only gone to the loo, after chatting with Peggy, and on her return, not a peep could she get out of her! A doctor came to certify the body, and four young policemen with a makeshift coffin carried her away.

By this time the nightman was flitting around like a pipistrelle bat. Tina asked him to arrange large pots of tea and biscuits on the house, to calm the old folk, and send

144

them back to bed. The party left to return to Wales in the morning.

Tina had two very nice Brazilian chambermaids, Cara and Clara, who were allocated the bedrooms on that section. In the morning, when her staff arrived for work, Tina informed these particular girls that one old lady had died overnight in room fourteen. She wouldn't be travelling in the coach soon to depart, but had already left, for a place unknown. Both girls were Catholics, and also very superstitious. Cara looked quite shaken, saying, 'There is something sadistic in that room, I cannot clean it any more!'

Clara was of the same opinion. Their fear was genuine, although Tina found it rather odd.

But there is an answer to every problem. She simply swopped the maids around. As most sections were alike regarding the workload her two students from Switzerland were happy to swap. Tina told them that there was no ghost. The only likely thing to occur was a cuckoo to jump from the wall, to announce that it was their lunchbreak. And with that they felt right at home!

Half of the top floor was a staff wing, and the other half for paying guests, with lovely views over the sea.

Tina had found a lovely antique stand and a heavy porcelain vase among some junk in a storeroom. she polished the wood to a high gloss and made a nice flower arrangement.

She figured that the old ladies would find it a welcoming and a homely touch, but some of the lads found other uses for it!

Late on a Saturday night, she was already in bed and heard a heated argument, when they got out of the lift. And before you know it, it developed into fisticuffs. The barmen, who had worked at the disco, accused the food and beverage managers of not sharing 'the kitty', and that they had been short-changed.

Tina heard her table being smashed up, and its legs used as weapons! without a second thought, she jumped out of bed and waded into the mêlée. She didn't mind the fighting, but objected very strongly to having her efforts destroyed. They knew about Tina's prowess in judo, and all ran to their respective rooms. All her pretty flowers had their necks broken and were trampled underfoot. She found a dustpan and brush in the cleaner's cupboard to sweep up the debris. But she wasn't going to let the chaps off so lightly. On Monday she made a collection from them, enough to buy a quality vase, and a bunch of cut flowers. And none of them protested!

One Sunday she was standing by her window, watching people on a crowded beach, and who should she spot? There was Theo sitting with a woman, this time someone a bit more mature, right opposite the hotel! Tina was aware that he kept track of her movements, but was this just a coincidence or was he hoping to bump into her at the seaside? When he was abroad, he expected an up to date report as to whether she had been seen in the company of any man. Although the KGB had given up on her, she was now being watched because of Theo's perverted jealousy.

Tina had a phone call one day from a general manager of one of the larger and more upmarket hotels, saying, 'I have heard about you, would you not prefer to work for us, it would be on a higher salary.'

She went along and had a very nice meeting with the general manager, but the job offer was for a permanent post, not seasonal. Tina declined because she really had to go back to London in the autumn, to be closer to her son. But something positive sprang from her interview with the rival hotel. When her employer got to hear about it, he promptly offered her a weekly 'backhander', and pressed a £10 note into her hand, as a starter!

One week Tina met him twice in the public areas, when he

stopped her for a brief chat, and gave her the retainer for the second time. Yes, well and good, he could well afford to!

The end of the season was approaching fast. Mrs Marks invited Tina to spend the winter as her houseguest in Florida. It was very sweet of her to offer, given that they had only known one another for five months. Sadly, Tina wasn't one to live at someone else's expense. She had always had to fend for herself, and others too!

She came to see Tina off on the train to London, leaving her address, should Tina change her mind.

41

Tina didn't visit Paul quite so often now that he was living with the foster parents, only once a month or so. And they would visit her in return, when Tina cooked a dinner for them. She had never fully come to terms with being apart from Paul, especially when passing a school playground, where children of the same age were skipping and playing. It would bring tears to her eyes, not being able to share in his daily life, wondering whether he was bullied, or if he was happy at his school. She never got to meet his teachers or school friends.

It became almost a phobia, and she would avoid such reminders and walk a long way round if she had to.

She met a number of eligible men, who would have been keen to have a permanent relationship but her experience with Theo had been so traumatic that she was unwilling to share a daily domesticity, and get emotionally entangled. She liked men's company in small doses, but chose to miss out on the benefits of having a partner, spending lonely nights at home.

She tried to find solace in her work and surroundings, and kept her personal life private. She met Melvyn occasionally at a tea dance at the Café de Paris, and now realised that he was harbouring designs of turning their friendship into a more serious relationship. But since a rich man had let her down so badly, Tina wondered whether a genuine millionaire would be too overwhelming.

On her return to London, she got a position as executive

head housekeeper in a very large hotel in west London, where she had a staff of seventy-three in her department. Although such a large operation, Tina felt that it was very well organised. The management team were all in their mid-twenties, and very enthusiastic. There were a lot of romances between them and the reception staff.

The managing director went one step further, and married a tour rep for Swedish groups. She actually had offices rented in the hotel premises.

Tina's large crew of chambermaids were married women living locally, most of them from Egypt or Morocco. They were such workhorses they could tackle any amount of work and bedmaking in the course of their day.

When she handed out their weekly wagepackets on Fridays, there were a few who couldn't write their name in the wages book, but acknowledged it by making a cross. One of them, Mrs Shaba, sent her a Christmas card titled: 'To my dear wife': now, that was a new one, but they do say that it's the thought that counts.

Her seven housekeepers were Australian, English and Irish, all under thirty. Tina hardly ever used casual staff, as she felt that their output wasn't economical. However, on this particular morning, due to the flu season, she needed two maids to fill a gap. She rang the labour exchange, which provided casuals for hotels. The two women that turned up were both in their fifties, one Yugoslavian, and the other, Mrs Flintstone, Irish. The floor housekeepers took them up to their work stations, and got them started with the job in hand.

In the late afternoon, Tina was sitting in her basement office with the door open doing her paperwork, when she heard her name shouted over and over. She couldn't work out where it came from, as it seemed to echo. She went along the passage to investigate, and heard a scuffle in the lift, doors opening and closing. And there was one of the casuals, Helga, strangulating her supervisor, Paulette! Oh, but she was vicious, like a wild beast holding onto her catch. All the maids had a long metal chain around their waist, for their room keys. This woman had wound her chain around Paulette's neck, and was still pulling! Tina found it a horrid sight, and was so angry that she had no choice but to manhandle the casual labour so that she would let go of her victim. Helga was tall, about Tina's size, but older. Tina's strength flowed forth and she shook the woman like a rabbit by the scruff and held her so tight, close to her windpipe, that her feet barely touched the ground from the lift to her office. She must have thought that she was in the claws of a lion! She left her keys, grabbed her bag and ran out. She never claimed her wages for that day, nor did she turn up at the labour exchange after that. Had she any sense, she had probably left the country.

Tina had yelled to the linen staff to escort Paulette to sit down, and give her some water. Since the culprit had run out, Tina went to see how bad Paulette's condition was. The chain had actually cut into her throat, drawing blood, and her neck looked discoloured and swollen. Paulette couldn't speak, only croak. She was checked over by a doctor, who gave her something for the shock. Luckily, Paulette's sister worked at the hotel as well, so Tina paid a minicab from petty cash to take them home.

After only four days' rest, Paulette was back at work, her neck first black, then every colour of a rainbow, but well covered by a chiffon scarf. Paulette was a very striking girl, with red hair and green eyes, and very good at her work.

When Tina wondered how she managed to take it all in her stride, Paulette explained: 'My Arabic boyfriend beats me up regularly, so I am no stranger to violence!'

Now it was Tina's turn to be shocked, giving her viewpoint on the subject: 'You should leave him at once, there are plenty more fish in the sea; more deserving someone with your looks and personality.'

Strangely, she did just that, but the fellow kept hounding her, and Tina lost her best housekeeper. Paulette and her sister Petula went to work for Hilton Hotels in Holland.

It took Tina a while to forget that sight in the lift. An attempted murder – another few seconds and it would have been just that.

The other casual turned out to be a disappointment as well, but in a rather different sort of way. Maids finished at four-thirty p.m. when they all trooped into the housekeeping office, to hand in their keys and sign out. Mrs Flintstone was the last one in the line and Tina wondered how she managed to find her way there at all. On the opposite side of Tina's desk, she promptly sat down, looking rather worse for wear. All the housekeepers were still at the office, some changing out of their uniforms in the back room, when Mrs Flintstone hit the floor, face down!

At first, Tina figured that the poor dear had fainted, being such a lightweight, not more than seven stone at the most. But in trying to revive her, Tina realised that the woman was drunk! When she was sat up again, her eyes rolling, Tina enquired, 'How did you manage to get so drunk?'

'Had miself a swig from every bottle, as I worked from one room to the other!' came a feeble answer.

No way could she have managed to walk to the tube or the bus station. So Tina decided to send her off in style, back to the labour exchange in Denmark Street. They were open until five-thirty p.m. So she would get there in time to present herself! First she rang for a minicab, for the second time that day, and asked two houseporters to support her to the street and place her in the back seat. She rang the agency, to say that Mrs Flintstone had a somewhat eventful day, and was on her way to their office to tell them about it!

She asked her floor supervisor to stay overtime to check the rooms that were allocated to Mrs Flintstone, in case she had missed something or left things undone. Tina felt that in

151

the last hour or two she hadn't managed any bedmaking at all. All the housekeepers offered to stay behind, to make light work on the check and any work needing to be done. Tina also asked them to make a note of any bottles out in the open, should there be any complaints. The German and Swedish chaps were in the habit of bringing a good supply of duty-free on arrival!

At five twenty-five p.m. there came a call from the labour exchange. The minicab driver had carried Mrs Flintstone into the office and they all found it absolutely hilarious!

But Tina's sentiments were not in agreement. She informed the caller that she wouldn't require their services in future, as the whole thing was not hilarious but utterly diabolical!

The housekeepers didn't come down until six, having had to change towels and remake some of the beds, and also finish Paulette's section. They were all starving by then, and were a truly great team, pulling together for the common good. Tina decided to thank them by taking them all for dinner at a nearby Italian restaurant, saying, 'Ladies, I don't know about you, but I reckon that on this particular day, we have been truly jinxed!'

In October, she had employed two Mormon girls, Marsha and Marissa, from Canada, who seemed happy in their work, and good at it. In December, she had a most unusual request from The White House Hotel. A personnel manager was on the line saying, 'I have heard that you have very well-trained staff, any chance of lending me six of your maids just for a week to cover for the Christmas rush?'

Tina promised to ask her girls, and get back to him later the same day. She caught them all together at lunchtime in the canteen, and put the proposition to them.

'Anyone willing to work near Regent's Park, lovely location, nice uniform provided and a bit of extra money.'

She got enough offers for a team of six, others

volunteering to work on their day off, to cover for the absentees!

Tina rang back to say that she had a willing team: two Australians, two Canadians and two Irish girls.

The following morning, earlier than usual they all turned up in Tina's office, like soldiers on parade to ask her, 'Do we look all right?'

Tina's heartstrings were pulled in admiration. 'Of course you do, how else would I be sending you on the mission!' She added that they were expected to go straight to The White House.

Then one of them asked, 'Is it part of the same group as this hotel?'

Tina was very economical with the truth, saying, 'Sort of. Anyway, you should fare okay for just a week!'

Three days later it was the executive housekeeper on the phone asking Tina, 'Can I keep your girls on permanently?'

She asked the lady to tell her girls to pop over to see her about it on their way home.

Four of them were keen to come back, but the two Mormons were quite happy to stay a bit longer. Tina informed The White House of the development.

In the Christmas week she received a card from them: 'Dear madam, here is hoping that you will very soon recall us.'

The poor things were under an impression that they were with the same company, only in a different location. Tina had been very naughty to mislead them, to do a favour for an entirely different group. However, five years later, she recalled that favour, not in casual maids but a catering crew of six for a dinner session.

In 1982, Tina was working in a north London hotel as the housekeeper in charge and catering supervisor. She returned from two weeks' holiday in Ibiza to learn that a relief manager, who was a son of a bitch and an imbecile, had upset the staff so much that they were all returning to France. They were waiting for Tina with their suitcases packed, to say goodbye and thank you for being so tolerant with their less than perfect English. They were well brought up youngsters and had been loyal to her. That relief man was always creeping around, looking for work, as he didn't do too well anywhere, and wasn't too much in demand. But to cock things up to such an extent! Tina was vexed, to say the least and it was not the best of homecomings!

A dinner party was booked for the top brass from Lord's Cricket Club, and she needed an experienced crew. She requested five waiters and a head waiter. The personnel department remembered Tina well after all these years, although they had never met in person, and her request would be granted. 'The head waiter will be wearing a tail coat!'

Tina remarked fondly, 'But not a top hat, they won't be going to Ascot!'

In that same hotel she carried on with a neighbourly goodwill, by borrowing a ten-litre container for a milk machine, leaving an IOU note, in token promise to return the same. And the neighbours in return borrowed champagne when their wedding party ran out. But no more lending out staff!

42

While working at the west London hotel, one day Tina popped to the shops and bumped into Theo. He had an armful of drycleaning, and was staying in a hotel locally, but flying back to the Middle East the next day.

He had come for a cataract operation at Moorfields Hospital. He didn't mention the outcome of their divorce hearing but appeared 'a man of the world', looking down on Tina as being in a humdrum job, working in a hotel. Such was his arrogance, that's how he saw it!

In fact, that was the last time they met, Tina's parting remark being, 'There may come a day when you find yourself wanting.'

All the young managers were leaving around the same time, as they had a fixed-term contract. Tina felt that a smooth running of operations and rapport was gone with them, and decided to do likewise. She was longing to be somewhere quiet in a country setting, and cooler during hot summers. She found a position on the Kent borders, in a privately-owned hotel, half the size of the last one. Tina liked the location, being surrounded by green parkland, offering pleasant walks away from traffic.

The staff and even some of the guests were more informal, and there was a lot of gossip going on about one thing and another. Tina began to notice how they were all 'at it'! Was there something in the air, soil or water that made everybody so amorous? One of the housekeepers remarked, 'At a certain spot of the common, seven winds meet!' Tina reckoned that must be the answer.

There was one guest, booked in for two weeks' stay. She never saw him, but according to the reception staff he was very handsome and smartly dressed. For three days running the chambermaid ran to her office in a flap, not knowing where to start, asking Tina to come and see herself. She found a double bed base propped against one wall, his mattress against the other and they were too heavy for the maid to put back in place.

After three days, Tina decided to teach him a lesson in the nicest possible way! She couldn't figure out what the man was doing in that room: aerobics or skateboarding?

She played a prank on him by making his bed 'a French sack', folding the top sheet over in the centre, and tucking the other under the pillows, making it impossible to get in, as the fold prevented your feet getting through.

The maid got all excited, wondering, what on earth Tina was doing. She asked the maid to learn from her, but never do it to a guest without her permission. She signed a compliment slip, and left it on his pillows! She expected protests, but nothing happened and he behaved like any other guest after that.

On her day off, she usually went to the West End to do some shopping, or go to a tea dance at the Café de Paris. On her return, in time to join the other staff at the restaurant for dinner, she learned that the managing director himself had gone around the floors, to keep an eye on the housekeeping staff. And what did he find. One of her maids, a rather flirty French girl, and a houseporter 'at it' and doing it in a guest bedroom! Tina felt, that there were too many sex maniacs about; or perhaps she herself was 'out of step' for not joining in.

On one of her ventures to go dancing, she encountered Jimmy, who was one of Melvyn's gang. Tina told him that she was now living not far from him. Jimmy had a garage in Greenwich, and he mentioned that Melvyn was always asking after her.

The following week she got a call from him, and an invitation for lunch. He was calling on Jimmy around midday the next day, and wouldn't want to miss her, being in the neighbourhood. Tina very much wanted to see him too, but could take only an hour for lunch.

There was a week-long conference at the hotel, and a lot of late departures. So she invited him to come for lunch at the hotel.

Melvyn wasn't giving up on her, but tried a new tack. Tina would have never imagined him as another headhunter, but that is exactly what he had in mind! He had seen a motel close to a motorway junction, and it would give him a daily cashflow as his money was tied up in commercial property.

He offered Tina a job to manage it, saying, 'You are the only one that I can trust; since it's a new venture for me, should I clinch the deal.'

They had known each other for a number of years socially, so Tina couldn't picture herself working for him. Rather than turn him down, she suggested something that he would surely refuse.

'I will only do it as a working partner,' she said.

Of course, being a shrewd business tycoon, he didn't appear too keen, which was what Tina hoped for.

That Christmas season Tina managed to take a fortnight off, and went to Majorca all by herself, since the few friends that she had all had other plans. On the evening she was to fly out, it got really foggy. The plane couldn't take off from Gatwick, so they were sent by coach to Luton airport, only to find it fogbound too. By then, the Gatwick area was clearing, and the plane took off at five a.m. During this toing and froing, she made friends with two Indian sisters from Birmingham. They spent their days together, going on tours to markets, and discos in the evenings, which was great, as Christmas spent alone can be a very sad time, whether at home or abroad. On her return in the early hours, she found breakfast trays still uncollected in the corridors. The staff had been very lax. Tina wasn't amused, and would tell them so!

43

Mama had been writing of being unwell and tired. Tina was very concerned, not knowing the reason, and always remembering her in good health and robust. In fact, she couldn't recall one day that mama had taken to her bed in her whole lifetime!

Tina took another holiday at Easter, this time with a girlfriend, and went to Tenerife. Although it was late March, it was a real scorcher and they needed loads of suncream and aftersun lotion. Then a storm broke and by this time they were digging sand from their ears as everyone was caught unawares sunbathing on the beach!

Even the lights went, and candles came out all around. On their first night out at a late night club, where the manager was a very affable Swedish chap, Tina met another sailor, Aaron from Argentina, who was a retired captain of a merchant ship, and had visited the port of Liverpool often during his career. He was living somewhere in the mountains in Tenerife, growing bananas. He looked very suave, with his silver-grey hair and expensive suits. Best of all was that he didn't expect anything in return for nightly entertainment, food and drink. Tina's room-mate was always welcome along, when Aaron came to pick them up at their hotel. It suited her so well, as she didn't believe in holiday romances.

On her return, Tina got another letter from mama, who had been in a hospital to have an operation for cancer, but too late, as it had spread too far. After this, she had to stay in the same hospital for four days every three weeks, to have radiotherapy. Even then, her letters continued to be humorous, so Tina prayed that perhaps it wasn't so bad after all, that she might even recover.

Tina sent her flowers through Interflora, which she would receive on her arrival at the hospital.

She had sold all the farm animals, as she wasn't able to manage the dairy operation. Tina thought it wise, as mama had done far too much in her lifetime, and should take it easier, being over sixty.

Sadly, mama's condition deteriorated, and she went into a nursing home. In her letter from there she showed concern for her old friend, Kirsty, who was visiting. She was in good health, but mama was sorry to see her hands so red and calloused. Still, no complaints of herself being in pain. However, Tina could understand her observation about someone's hands, as she kept hers smooth by using glycerine- and alcohol-based hand lotions, and had taught Tina to do likewise. In her book, hard or rough work was no excuse for chapped hands; one had to take more time and care in looking after them.

Thinking about her, Tina eased her mind by writing a poem:

Only to Mama

Only to mama, I recite this song,
as from the time we met, is far too long.
The distance is far, past the ocean and land,
but for all you taught me, I am ever so glad.

Only to mama, I am thankful for this,
the guidance I followed with memories.

For all I've seen and done, through the years,
I wrote in the letters, and told on the phone,

to reassure you, mama, that astray I haven't gone.
Many a temptation I survived, and evil traps cast aside.
That advice of yours, held me on the straight and narrow!

Only to mama I am grateful for this,
trying to fill her every wish.

In the tragic years, as I recall the past,
When the war was on, in the world so vast,
you lost my father, whom I have never seen,
only his photo, of what had been.
Just me, only an infant then,
to take his place, but never replace.

With loving care, and a code of rules,
you brought me up to womanhood!

Only to mama, who survived this,
I pray and bless her for her braveness.

It was in early May when Tina found a black-edged telegram among her mail left on her desk. She learned that mama had passed on in the nursing home at the age of sixty-eight. In such homes, burials are arranged with great speed. The funeral was to be two days from her opening the telegram. It came as a shock, as mama never let on how ill she was. Perhaps to the very end she felt compassion for Tina and her own problems.

Tina sent a wreath, as she couldn't arrange to fly over at such short notice. It was so sad that mama couldn't enjoy some rest in her beautiful country surroundings, but as it was, it was better not to linger in pain. It must have been God's will to release such 'a good one', and none more deserving of peace.

Tina didn't go dancing for some time, instead she found

161

her long solitary walks in leafy parkland very therapeutic to reflect on one's life and destiny! Also getting immersed in her daily work and all that it entailed. Ups and downs, but never dull nor boring.

Soon it was another Christmas. Tina had given a month's notice to leave just before the holidays, as she planned to have a break in the sun before starting a new job in north London.

She had found the distance from the West End a bit of an obstacle, and missing the last train from Charing Cross was expensive as she had to pay a minicab. Also, the attraction in her new job was that she was to have her own flat, away from her work, but still only walking distance from the hotel.

44

She settled in happily, and was able to entertain her friends, since she was able to cook and have a more homely lifestyle. Paul and his new family came to dinner occasionally. Tina worked long days, as she was now involved in catering operations as well as managing the housekeeping.

Her core staff had been there for some years before and stayed throughout, which was a great relief. Except for the fact that they expected long holidays, at home in Spain or Portugal. Tina went along with their wishes, knowing that she could bank on their loyalty on their return. There has to be some give and take in a good working relationship. Furthermore, she had no hassle in finding relief staff, she had students queueing at the back door to step in!

By this time Tina was aware that some people in her age group were on the lookout for a husband for the second time around. Like hers, their first marriage had failed, but for quite different reasons. Tina wasn't on the lookout, but enjoyed observing the goings on; once was more than enough for her!

She remarked to one lady, who was getting desperate, 'Best you can hope for is somebody else's leftovers!'

So why the fuss? As after first marriages there are often children to consider, and for men alimonies and maintenance to pay. Things had changed since they were all chasing their first romance. And there were some who were permanently on the lookout; perhaps they were not cut out for matrimony in the first place and were somewhat suspect.

Tina enjoyed her work, surrounded by oil paintings and oriental rugs. She was also comfortable in her flat, and often had her friends to stay over the weekends.

Paul was ten years old that summer, and wanted to see mummy's homeland, and to meet his Uncle Leo and Auntie Irene, not forgetting his cousins, Petri and Folkke. Tina made arrangements to fly over for a fortnight, and also to take Paul's house-brother Danny, to keep him company, should he not find English-speaking playmates.

But Tina had yet another obstacle to overcome. Because Paul was a ward of court she had to obtain permission from the Home Secretary to take her own son out of the country! Still, it was a small price to pay for the security of knowing that Theo couldn't snatch him away to the Middle East. Then she would have surely lost him, as Theo had threatened when Tina withdrew his meal ticket.

They flew from Heathrow to Helsinki, and travelled from there by coach to sister Irene's apartment. They planned to spend the holiday on the farm, but there was a message from Leo saying that he didn't want any visitors who didn't speak Finnish.

Tina was very upset for the sake of the boys, but didn't let on; she was going to deal with Leo on her own. His attitude was too arrogant for her liking, after all a third of the farm was hers, as mama had willed equally between the three of them.

Tina had visited in the late summer after mama's funeral in May, and stayed at the farm with Leo alone. She had found the stillness very strange at first; no dairy herd sounds, not even any pets, no cat or dog!

Leo wanted an easy life, and had rented all the arable land to neighbouring farmers. Tina wasn't offered her share of the proceeds. She also got suspicious that a certain section of the woodland looked rather sparse. She had put her wellies on and gone to take a closer look. She observed a large number of fresh tree stumps, felled during the previous winter. Leo was very evasive, saying that it was simply clearance ordered by the Forestry Commission. Tina knew this to be a straight lie, she also asked around the neighbours about Leo's activities during the winter months. They confirmed Tina's suspicions that he had sold a large amount of timber. Not only that, she followed heavy tyre tracks into a barn which was some distance from the homestead. Although the double doors were padlocked, she could peep through the gaps in the walls, to see it stacked high with planks, freshly cut at the sawmill, ready to sell to building merchants.

Tina realised that Leo was doing very well financially, acting as if he was now sole owner of the farm, whereas he should have shared with Irene and Tina equally.

45

The folk in the village were a very closely-knit community, helping each other, especially at harvesting time, when the neighbouring farmers moved from one house to another, as a large group, to make light of a day's work.

Every season of the year was so clearly defined, and tasks planned accordingly. It was almost like a production line.

Curtains were changed twice a year, and so were the windows! Before Easter, heavy-lined curtains came down, to be stored in the attic. The inner windows were removed likewise, so that the outer frames could be opened in the warm weather. Not only that, but in the summer, yet another frame was slipped into the double frame, which wasn't glass, but fine meshwire netting, to keep the flies out. For the summer, the curtains were light flowery cotton, bringing the sunshine in!

In October, when the night frosts set in and days grew short, the heavy curtains were put back, plus the double-glazed windows. Often cotton-wool or matchboxes were used to absorb any condensation. Before Easter, or at the latest before May Day, all the rugs were taken to a river or sometimes to the lakes to be shampooed. This outing was regarded as a day's picnic, as it took place away from the farm. The neighbouring women would make a day's outing of it, as a mini-break from the usual chores. They had a chance to tuck into their hampers, and exchange village gossip!

In late May, when the grass was long enough, the cows

were let out into the pasture. They would jump for joy, like newborn lambs, till they wore themselves out, and calmed down!

This was followed by yet another community effort, moving from one farm to the next. A gang of women and children would 'get stuck in' to wash out and then lime-wash the concrete stalls in the cowsheds.

And the same was done in the vegetable cellars, in the later summer. All the compartments were cleared of any rotting potatoes or beets and then washed out, and left to air before the next produce was stored for the winter.

As far back as Tina could remember, mama taught her children that to waste was to sin. Every possible thing was recycled. Newspapers were tied up with string, and a van would go around the farms once a month to collect them for the paper factories. Old woollen socks, jumpers and mittens were never thrown out, no matter how tatty; they were washed, and again collected to be recycled in a factory to make new blankets. Any returnable bottles had a deposit in the shops, so the children were very keen to take them back for some pocket money. As for leftover food, needless to say it was collected for the pigs and chickens.

Coming to work in hotels, Tina found it very hard to get used to seeing so much food, especially bread, being thrown into the rubbish bin. In some of the hotels she instigated a twice-weekly collection by pig farmers. But the problem in the hot weather was the flies, and strong smells after a missed collection. As for the farmers, they weren't too happy finding handfuls of paper serviettes among their pigfeed, and an occasional piece of cutlery!

Mama's good teaching left such a mark on Tina that to this day she cannot throw away any bread, unless it's mouldy. She will always take it to the birds in a park or any garden square.

As Tina pointed out, her village neighbourhood was a

friendly and cooperative community, except for one rotten apple in the basket. That particular farmer, Ossi, was so bad that he was shunned by all the men around for miles. He was a known deserter, hiding in the woods when the rest of the men fought for their country. If that wasn't bad enough, he also made bootleg hooch, getting raving drunk on raw spirits.

As a young girl, Tina had come upon his illicit distillery by a stream, deep in the woods, while berry-picking. He made it with corn, sugar and yeast. It was of course an offence, and anyone caught ended up in prison for a long stretch.

However, his long-suffering wife was well liked, and received a lot of sympathy from everyone. She never complained, and accepted her fate, as if it was her lot in life to struggle and scrimp with no hope of it ever getting better. She had nine children to look after, clothe and feed, and her husband was so irresponsible that any money coming from the dairy was spent on boozing.

The younger children got into the habit of running to Tina's mama daily. Her being so generous by nature, she sent them home with two hot loaves under their arms. Even their dog got into the act, and became a daily visitor for something to eat!

Mama was fascinated by Tina's choice of words when describing Ossi, making it known just how bad he was. He would walk around the borderline of his fields, inspecting the crop as an excuse to come in for a visit when it was coffee time after dinner, when he was sure to find a listening audience. Often Tina would pour the coffee and pretend that the pot was empty, and leave 'the sod' without, so strong was her detestation of the man!

Because there wasn't 'a man of the house', he saw the home as his last bastion where he could go. Mama had a lot of patience, but even she couldn't tolerate what he did during one of his drunken binges, after which he was barred from their house.

One summer's night he had gone with his eldest son to a farm in the next village, where there was an older son, about the same age as Arvi. They had all got sloshed on illicit spirits, and got into a fight. Ossi had hit the farmer's son Olli with a large stone and killed him. He persuaded his eldest, Arvi, to admit to murder so that he wouldn't have to go to prison, having previous form as well!

The boys, especially Arvi, hated their father so much that prison seemed an attractive option to get away from home! And his sacrifice paid off, as during such a long stretch he learned the skill of landscape gardening.

When he got out, he married well, as everyone knew him to be totally innocent. The worst part of that family was the fact that they should have been quite comfortable, with four young men to work the farm, but as there was no leadership, the lads got odd jobs elsewhere.

Tina had started to make plans to go back to Finland and run the farm as mama had done. But she learned that since 1973, the laws of dual nationality had been changed. As Tina was now a British subject, she had forfeited her nationality and could live in Finland only six months a year. Perhaps it was just as well, as she wouldn't have been able to take Paul with her, although she didn't discover this until the following summer.

Although there was an indoor swimming pool in the apartment complex where sister Irene lived, the hot weather and cramped living arrangements for three extra people wasn't really what Tina had planned for the boys. Irene was a member of a Civil Service holiday centre by Lake Saimaa. Tina asked her to book a week's stay for all of them, for which she agreed to pay. So, they had a train journey right across the country from the south-west border to the south-east, which gave Paul and Danny an opportunity to see lots of farms and animals. The holiday centre was well away from any shops and traffic, with chalet bungalows dotted in the

169

woods by the lake, plus a restaurant, sauna and recreation facilities. There was a very popular open-air dancefloor, where Irene stayed late at night, snogging with a border guard, while Tina and the boys had been asleep long since, before she crept in!

46

Nothing much bothered Leo, except for such a big man he was scared of thunder and gypsies. They would call at the farms once a year, with a horse and cart, full of women and children, selling bakeware made of tin. If you didn't buy any or give them money they would put all sorts of curses on the families. As they were real Romanies, Leo took them seriously.

During the short but very hot summer, when it often didn't rain for five or six weeks, the severe thunderstorms would create a build up of electricity in the air. A lightning bolt often travelled along the electricity cables and struck the junction boxes, situated on the walls of outbuildings. Being wooden structures or barns full of dry hay, this could cause fierce fires.

Leo was prepared. When dark clouds gathered, and he felt a headache coming on, he would pull his wellies on and go into the cellar until it had passed over!

Tina found a Finnish lawyer in Fleet Street to act on her behalf in selling her share of the legacy. Since Leo had snubbed the boys and herself, she didn't wish to confront him in person. She had a survey and valuation done, by signing four copies of attorney, including a lawyer and a bank manager in Finland. Letters were passing to and fro. Leo and Irene couldn't agree on the price of buying Tina's share.

That's when she decided to play on Leo's fear of gypsies. She instructed her lawyer to send a letter in which she proposed to sell out to Romany gypsies. So Leo would have some lively company, with little ragged 'kiddies' running hither and thither, likely to take a fancy to his motorbike!

Well, it worked. Leo would have paid any price to avoid Tina's proposition. In truth, she wouldn't have known where to find any Romanies, but Leo wasn't in the know!

Once her money came through, there was no further contact between herself and her siblings! In fact, they didn't have much in common, since mama was no longer at the helm. Tina often wondered how twins could be so different.

Sister Irene was a quick-tempered livewire. Her life since her marriage continued as it began, struggling financially and emotionally. Thankfully her boys were her 'port in the storm'.

Leo was blasé and laid back, he could sleep all day, be it in the barn or the farmhouse! He only had to dip into his 'mine of green gold' and to cut down some more prime trees for an instant cashflow!

On Tina's last visit, Kirsty came to see her on an old bicycle. Leo had told her previously that she had bought a cottage some five kilometres from the farm and that it was crammed with any old junk and old newspapers. No doubt she too wanted to hang on to her memories, sad as they were.

Tina reminded her of mama's promise long ago, that the farm could be her home, if she so wished. But Kirsty liked her independence, and would continue to call regularly to do the cleaning and the laundry, but Leo would have to do his own cooking since he had all the time in the world!

The chef at Tina's hotel was Austrian, and her good cooking and baking was such a temptation that all the dancing and long workdays weren't enough to prevent her putting on weight. This wouldn't do at all, so the following winter Tina booked into a health farm for a fortnight to go on a fast!

She had sampled three different ones, the one in Suffolk being her favourite, and the only one where she could go on a five-day fast, having nothing, except a flask of boiling water with a dollop of honey and a slice of lemon. This was brought to her room first thing in the morning, and left on her bedside table in the evening. During the day she was allowed either a plain yoghurt or fresh fruit, half a pear or a slice of melon, and lots of barley water to drink between her treatments!

The only proper meal that she had was the night before leaving, which was a sit-down affair in the dining room, with a glass of their homemade wine.

She thrived on it, except sometimes she needed salt tablets for stiff legs and knee-joints.

There was a doctor to check everyone on arrival, to establish whether they were fit enough to go on a fast. She had a programme slip every morning for appointments, telling her what treatment rooms she was to attend. She had hand massage and underwater massage with a power hose on alternate days, and steam cabinet treatment followed by icy water jets! There was a Turkish sauna and a dry sauna, where they were bolted in for a specified length of time. Halfway through the session they all trooped out 'in the nuddy', young and old alike, to be rubbed all over with coarse sea salt, and rinsed off under a cold shower. After the second session, with scented and wet paper napkins over their noses, they were expected to jump into an icy pool.

On one occasion there was a very attractive lady, much younger than Tina, who jumped in front of her, and fainted clean out from the shock of the icy cold! Still, there were plenty of attendants to pull her straight out.

After the pool, they all had to lie down for ten minutes, to calm their heartbeat.

But one felt so alive, and yet relaxed after this 'regimental palaver'!

On her very first visit there in 1970, Tina made friends with a lovely old lady in her mid-seventies, who was 'fit as a fiddle'. Her elderly husband telephoned daily to say that their parrot was driving him up the pole shrieking, 'Where is Vera?'

One day he turned up, having driven a long distance there and back with the parrot cage, to show the bird where Vera was. It paid off. After their visit, the bird shut up!

On her second visit there, when Tina was in her dressing-gown waiting to be called to a steam cabinet, two ladies asked her for an autograph. She was totally at a loss as to what for, saying, 'But I am a nobody!' She then learned from them that there was a guest from Eastern Europe who was a duchess, now living in France, and that she was tall, youngish, and had red hair. Although Tina was naturally blonde, occasionally she experimented with other shades and this time the colour of her hair was reddish!

The next day the duchess invited her to a local pub for a glass of wine, which Tina declined, but had a walk with the lady in the grounds instead. She found the whole thing a bit funny, although she admitted that they looked somewhat alike.

The duchess had encountered some problems trying to hide her oil paintings from tax inspectors. Tina commented that she had never had such hassles, having none to hide, and even her hair colour came from a bottle!

In the evenings they would enjoy yoga, or have educational lectures from the medical profession, showing slides of the human body, and talking of the importance of the correct posture and diet. At times they would adjourn to the TV lounge for a game of cards.

On this particular visit Tina was sitting in a conservatory by the indoor pool when an elderly gentleman asked permission to join her. He turned out to be another property tycoon from the Kensington area. In the course of their

174

conversation Tina mentioned having worked for Mr Collier in the late Sixties and early Seventies and that no doubt he knew of him.

He informed Tina that Mr Collier had died some two years earlier of a heart-attack. Both agreed that he had left his mark in his own way, each knowing what was referred to.

Tina herself had bumped into him when taking a shortcut between Kensington and Earl's Court, when she was managing the hostel there until 1976. He had a wide smile for her, and opened his shirtfront to show her a battery under the skin, saying, 'Now that I have a pacemaker, I cannot have girls any more!'

Tina's joky reply was: 'You old goat, you've had more than your fair share of oats, so what's to moan about?'

'Oh, you have turned into a hard woman!'

'Life itself has been a good teacher!' Tina had called over her shoulder. She didn't mention the cheque, having a sneaky feeling that Mrs Collier hadn't told her husband about it.

The other healthfarm where Tina spent a fortnight's break on two occasions was in Bedfordshire, and a totally different kind of place. There was no fasting, but a calorie-controlled diet and lots of activity to burn off excess fat. Most of the guests were younger, many of them sport and television personalities.

It was situated in very pleasant country surroundings. In the mornings, Tina joined in a brisk walk around a lake, which was a four-mile hike. After a few days, most dropped out, finding it too early to start and too fast a pace. But Tina stayed with the last few, as she found it a great way to start the day. On their return there was room service for a light breakfast, followed by aerobics and water ballet.

The days passed fast by keeping appointments for various treatments. Lunch was a buffet with a good choice of salads, and dinner was a three-course hot meal. There was one guest, very young, not more than twelve, and it was a grand place for him to spend part of his school break. His grandfather called in his yellow Rolls-Royce most evenings to have dinner with the lad. He was the type of a boy who kept an eye on all the goings on.

One day, when Tina was on a terrace sunlounger with a crowd of other guests, he came bearing some interesting news. An American gentleman had just arrived, asking for whisky and soda to be brought to his room.

'Sorry, sir, no alcohol, only minerals in the minibar!' the reception staff had informed him. The country air had given him an appetite, so he would have a juicy steak for his dinner!

'Sorry, sir, no red meat here!'

He had then begun to observe his surroundings; what kind of a country-house hotel was it? Mark, the lad, had been standing close, so as not to miss anything. Then the American had noticed scantily clad people wearing dressing gowns. 'Wow, is this place a high class brothel?'

The lad had been in fits of laughter telling the man, 'Lots of classy ladies here, but it's a health farm!'

Thus the misunderstanding was sorted out!

The gentleman had been attending a conference in London, which didn't last as long as he had expected. Having a few days before he was due to fly home, he had gone to Thomas Cook Travel Agents and asked to be booked into a real country house hotel with a pool and a good tennis court. Well, that's what he got, except the catering wasn't equal to a hotel. Mark kept the ladies informed that in the evening he booked a minicab to take him to Luton to have his steak, whisky and soda!

The next day he was getting into a swing of things, trying out massage by a woman. Tina was in the next cubicle, being pummelled by a young man, and they heard grunts and squeals like a piglet. The masseur ran out to her supervisor,

176

explaining that she couldn't do it because he was so hairy all over his back! Her fingers were pulling and getting tangled in his hairy coat and that's why he was yelping so much!

Tina couldn't stop laughing, so her masseur couldn't do much either, but that was no fault of his. She was so intrigued to see this man, and did so by the pool later on.

He was a giant of a man, and hairy like a monkey. After three days he had to leave, but reckoned that it was the best mini-holiday a man could get; he couldn't wait to tell the folks back home! And he gave the lad, Mark, a good time too, while it lasted!

Having meals during the stay, Tina normally lost eight pounds, whereas being on a fast she managed anything between nine and eleven pounds.

The third place that Tina had sampled was more of an activity centre, with treatments, with an à la carte restaurant with a bar. This was in North Wales, where she booked only for a week during her Easter break.

One day their party attempted to climb Snowdon. At a higher level they felt quite giddy, as the air was very pure but thin. They never reached the snow-covered top, and they kept slipping and sliding. Dusk and fog descended early, so they had to come down, which in fact was much harder than going up. Tina felt pins at the back of her knees and thigh muscles. On return to the home base, they all needed a good massage, a soak in the jacuzzi, followed by a sauna!

It was a very pleasant experience, and well suited to younger people.

47

She had settled nicely at the hotel, and before she realised it nearly five years had flown by. Then the proprietors informed all the staff that they were selling out as a going concern. Her employer asked Tina to stay put and look after her house, which she did for a while longer.

But once again, she felt that the rapport was missing, although her fellow staff were staying on quite happily. The Metropolitan Hotel Group had a subsidiary company called the Grand Met International Site Services, and Tina had answered their ad, and was called for an interview at their head office in Hammersmith. The job in question turned out to be in Algeria. A charming man there decided that someone like her would send the native workers into a flap. He was of an opinion that the particular job on a construction site really required a man. In fact, he had already seen a man from Poland, but there was a problem in obtaining the papers needed. But he was sure to find Tina a good position too, perhaps a bit closer to home.

The very next day, she received a telegram, stating: 'Urgently needed at the Texaco oil-rigs in Loch Kisshorn, please answer Yes or No; rail tickets will be posted forthwith, if affirmative?'

Now Tina wanted a bit of adventure, so after checking a map to establish where Loch Kisshorn was, she stored most of her belongings with a friend, so as to travel lightly such a long distance.

She received a very detailed contract, a pass to the

campsite, and a return ticket from Euston to Strathcarron. She was to travel overnight, and had a sleeper in the first-class section, and even morning coffee brought to her cabin. On reaching the end of their journey, they had to change to a slow, local train to Inverness, for another couple of hours, where a courtesy van was waiting for her and a few engineers returning from home leave.

As it was late autumn, the countryside looked desolate. On reaching a gate guard to present their papers, the men jumped from the van, but Tina saw the muddy ground, and wasn't going to get her black shoes all dirtied. What did she do? Called the guard to the van instead to check that her pass was in order!

The reception area and restaurant were set up as in any large hotel. She was introduced to her immediate boss, the facilities manager, whose assistant she was to become. He took her to a well-furnished three-bedroomed bungalow nearby that was to be her home. The sitting room was used by duty managers for a few hours on rest period. Next, they went for lunch, which was a lavish affair with lots to choose from. Tina met the managing director, who gave her some papers to sign and to join the union, as everyone else had. But no, she didn't believe in unions and would go solo, come hell or high water!

Talking of which, the sea was wild like a demon and the narrow road that they had traversed was really terrifying, with high waves crashing on one side and a solid rock wall on the other! Had she had a car there, she wouldn't have been brave enough to drive it.

The accommodation for the rig workers was a row of one-storey chalet blocks. There was also a recreation block, with shops, pubs, a cinema, a bank, a laundrette and a sports hall. Some of the men that she encountered had their arms covered in gory tattoos, and a tell-tale crewcut. Tina asked her boss whether they were what she suspected. Oh, yes, some were ex-cons all right!

179

She had really gone to an extreme this time, where hundreds of men roamed in a wilderness, with somewhat 'iffy' backgrounds! Still, it was an adventure, to start with. There was also a hospital on site, as the machinery was in operation round the clock and accidents were bound to happen, and some workers were hell-bent on starting a fight, when they had drunk too much during their off-duty period.

All the female staff were bussed to and from nearby villages, as none walked on that dangerous road. At night Tina was the only female, apart from nurses at the clinic, doing a night shift. She had to liaise between the facilities manager, housekeeping and the head of security. There was an incident when one of the housekeepers told her that there was a sandwich plate going from room to room in 'a Brown Block', finding it very odd. Together, they went to investigate and Tina's first reaction was that there was an intruder being fed light meals. In a wardrobe they found a redhead, a buxom woman cowering in a corner! She had been passed among some men in the same fashion as the telltale sandwich plate! The men, who had managed to smuggle her in were booted out, since they had breached security.

Tina and her boss even had to check two supply ships that called regularly with food and other items for the kitchen. One of the ships was Greek-registered and they had to go over the holds for drugs or any illegal substances. These trips were a time for hard hats and wellies!

The managing director's driver, Alistair, was very pleased to drive Tina to any shops, even as far as Inverness, where she observed snow-covered hills, and they would venture into a pub for 'a wee dram', to keep the chills off their bones!

Her contract was very specific about not fraternising with the 'crew', as her job was rather security sensitive. That left her somewhat isolated after work, and some nights she was on her own in the bungalow. Although it was close to the main block, the bedrooms faced woodland and wilderness. She was very wakeful, wondering who was tapping on the window. Was it a branch of a tree or was it an ex-convict out there in the dark?

She began to realise that her colouring and curves were a disadvantage in this particular setup!

Had it been summer with light evenings, it could have been quite pleasant, with sea-breezes, but in the winter season it was scary and wild! The terms of her contract were very generous: three weeks on duty, followed by one week's home leave, first class travel paid anywhere within UK, and a very high salary, by today's rates equal to £35,000 a year. On top of that, she had free housing and food, and no bills to pay, except taxes!

Sadly, it is one thing or the other, and Tina began to feel that sooner or later she could get raped, surrounded by such large number of men, so she decided to give up her high earnings and head back to London.

Once again she travelled overnight, arriving at Euston before seven a.m. She asked a taxi driver to head towards Sussex Gardens and once there to slow down so that she could check for any vacancy signs. She booked into a bed and breakfast for one night only to start with.

The landlord was an Irishman, who appeared to do most everything by himself. He offered her a good breakfast, for an extra payment, as she hadn't stayed the night before and wasn't over the moon about her Scottish money!

Around midday, she checked the papers for any job vacancies, and spotted a position for an assistant manager in another bed and breakfast in Norfolk Square, just five minutes' walk away. She arranged an interview with the manager and two proprietors. After a good night's sleep, she moved across the next day, eager and present for work!

The manager was a very handsome fellow, with a great

181

dress sense. On going out he would wear a polo-neck with a tan leather coat, or a red wool polo with a black leather jacket, plus a dark wool overcoat and a maroon scarf! All looked so elegant on him, being very dark, with jet-black hair. Cecil was Tina's age, born in South America, but had gone to school in Wales, and then to university there. He had held the post of chief accountant with a leading oil company for a number of years, but had fallen into a habit of excessive drinking, and had lost his job. After he was too ashamed to face his former colleagues and neighbours and moved to London to work in a live-in job.

His marriage had broken down because of his 'downfall'. However, his twelve-year-old son came to visit him as he wasn't prepared to visit his former home.

The hotel was very upmarket compared to the nearby guest houses. All sixteen bedrooms had private en-suite facilities, and were well furnished. The kitchen was fitted with a dishwasher. The bookings were confirmed in writing or by telex, so anyone calling at the door on the offchance wasn't able to get in. In fact, it was such a high standard that the previous year it had won an annual trophy from the Board of Trade and Commerce, as the best bed and breakfast hotel of the year! Tina and Cecil's accommodation were next door to each other at the rear of the basement, close to the kitchen. They worked well together, cooking and serving a full English breakfast, and organised the maids, laundry and shopping and banking. When either one had a day off, the proprietors came twice weekly to help with the cooking and the paperwork.

Both had enough time off, as they organised their hours to do either the early shift or the late one, until midnight. It was almost like having a husband, as they usually had their meals together, but it didn't take Cecil very long before he wanted to share the bed as well! Tina liked the man well enough, but it wasn't wise to mix business with pleasure. A solution was found. Cecil invited his ex-girlfriend from Wales to spend a weekend with him once in a while!

After her visits he was happy 'as a sandboy', and all was well for a while! The problem was that the lady was a married woman, and partly to blame for his marriage failing.

When the summer days dawned hot and sultry, and there was Cecil pestering her to get into his bed Tina decided to put some roots in her life. She had saved enough money working, plus her legacy, so she bought an upmarket flat. However, they remained friends, visiting one another and when it was her turn they would cook and eat dinner together at the hotel, where he remained quite happily. While still working in the locality, Tina heard that the Irish landlord where she had stayed just the one night, had been mugged.

A villain had hit him over the head with a stone near his hotel, thinking that he was carrying money to the bank. But, as it was, he was on his way to the butchers. Sadly, the blow had been so severe that he died two days later of a bloodclot to the brain.

It was very sad news in the community, as he was well liked and lived for his hotel. As to what happened to his business, being a single man, Tina had no further news of his affairs.

While looking for a suitable property, she learned a great deal. Cheaper ones on the market needed extensive works to be carried out, such as rewiring and upgrading the waterworks. Taking the additional cost and worry about shoddy workmanship, she opted for something more upmarket, and ready to move in. Also, she was concerned about the security, and wanted to be close to a tube station, rather than walking any dark side streets for any distance.

The flat that she bought was in exceptionally good order. The previous owner-occupier had been a newly-qualified architect who had been 'tinkering' day and night to put his talents into practice.

The wallcoverings were fabric instead of wallpaper. There were built-in units for wardrobes and drawers, pile carpets and dimmer lights. The kitchen was small, but very tastefully done, with heavy glass shelves above a breakfast bar, with chrome and white leather stools on both sides. There were no curtains, but blinds on heavy brass rails.

It was a man's flat in colour schemes, and needed very little furniture. Tina bought a five-seater sofa, including corner units, which were moveable, as foot-stools to match a green carpet.

When she moved in, a few neighbours living in the block wanted to take a look since it was regarded as show-flat!

There was twenty-four hour porterage and the service charges were quite low in comparison to some properties that she had viewed.

This time, Tina didn't look for a permanent position, when she would have to sign a contract. An ex-boyfriend made 'a beeline' to get her in between jobs and commitments, to help out in starting a business, in hopes of a partnership. She spent some time in Oxford helping with his proposed venture but had to earn enough to pay the mortgage and the bills.

She registered with a catering agency, doing temping, and for the first time she didn't have the responsibility of being in charge!

48

But two factors decided that she wasn't happy with her independence. For so many years she had lived 'on top of her work', and been closely involved with people she knew on a twenty-four hour basis. She had become so used to it that living alone and not knowing her neighbours she felt very isolated and lonely. Also, property prices were still going up at a very fast rate. There was a chap who was visiting a friend in the block and kept calling to take a look at Tina's flat, as he was very keen on getting his hands on it! In the end, she agreed to a private sale, including the contents. She lived there for only thirteen months, and had no definite plans as to what she would do next.

But as the prospective buyer was so keen to move in before Christmas, and she was to make a nice profit out of her venture into the property market, she agreed to sell out. That left her staying in a hotel over the holidays, but it was rather a novelty to be a guest rather than an employee.

This was not a time of year to check the job market; there would be time in the New Year. And, who knew, another 'headhunter' might pop up somewhere. This time it didn't happen however, as she was getting on in years, being over forty. Instead she had to deal with an unexpected obstacle. The buyer's surveyor had recommended her a solicitor who would conclude matters speedily. He did so, but turned out to be a crook!

Tina had received a lump sum of money before Christmas, but was waiting for the rest of it, after his fee and the final mortgage payments were settled. In January she received his invoice, and a cheque for £12,000. Tina paid it into her building society account, only to have it returned, bounced! Tina went to confront him at his office in Edgware, Middlesex, their first meeting face to face. She began to worry that there must be something really fishy, as the sign outside read 'Promotions', rather than 'Solicitors'. He gave Tina such a hard-luck story, having financial difficulties, having to pay private school fees for his two daughters, but said that his situation was temporary, adding, 'I really need your money for a few months, surely you aren't in a great hurry, being an independent lady?'

Tina's answer to that kind of bull is not for repeating. She called her solicitor a low-down conman, and wasn't willing to contribute to his school fees! He sent another cheque, which also bounced. This time Tina was on the warpath. She wasn't keen on a lengthy court case, so tried another tack. She took a minicab to Hendon police station, with the cheques, as a promise for payment, to show as evidence. She was fortunate to encounter a very helpful and professional DI, who took up her case.

'There is nothing that I loathe more than a bent solicitor, especially one on my home patch!' he enthused. He promised to investigate the man in question, and keep Tina up to date with developments. Within three days she received a computer printout about Mr Tucker being struck off the solicitors' roll three years earlier, and sacked from his last position for fraud!

And yet he was carrying on legal work under false pretences. DI Bird rang Tina saying that this time he would get a prison sentence. Tina asked him to pay him a visit, and put the fear of God into the villain. He had done just that, and Mr Tucker was getting panicky, saying that he would have to borrow the money from his elderly mother if Tina wasn't prepared to give him a few months to sort out his affairs.

Tina gave him twenty-four hours to come up with the money owed to her, plus the interest, from the date of contracts being exchanged. He then came to visit her, only to grovel, which gave her a chance to treat him with nothing but contempt, adding that she was ashamed to be in the company of a shark like him. Two hours before his time was up, the money was paid by a banker's draft to Tina's account! And all thanks to that brilliant DI Bird at the Hendon police station!

49

While she had to cope with this worry, she had started in a new position, working for an international housing charity and had a nice flat to go with the job.

She didn't keep in touch with Theo personally, but heard news occasionally from Paul and his foster parents. In the early Eighties he had returned from the Middle East when the war between Iran and Iraq had intensified to the point where Iraqi forces bombed the oil ports where he had been based. Due to political tensions in Iran, he couldn't get his money out of the country but was paid in uncut diamonds instead. He had to sell them at Hatton Gardens, at a loss having to pay duty.

At the time, he was living with a woman in Kingston, Surrey, until she kicked him out and he had settled in some rough neighbourhood in south-east London! Paul was growing so fast that Tina was sure that he would be over six foot tall, like his dad.

She encouraged him in his sporting activities, to keep him from getting involved in drinking or drugs. Thus he took part in mini-marathons for charities, went to Richmond ice rink regularly and enjoyed riding his racing bike, playing rugby and workouts in the local gym. Tina was more than willing to spend her last penny on buying him new skates and new tyres for the bike to keep up with 'his good innings'.

Tina had travelled abroad frequently, unusually twice a year to top up her tan. She had been to European countries and the Canary Islands a number of times. When Paul was seventeen, he asked to go with her. Tina's girlfriend wanted to come too as it was Christmas-time again. It was the first time that Tina booked a self-catering apartment rather than book two hotel bedrooms. Paul slept on the living room sofa, while the ladies shared a double bedroom. Once again, they were in Tenerife to enjoy the winter sunshine!

Paul made friends with a whole crowd of lads of his age from the word go! They were out all day and spent the nights at local discos. Most evenings they had dinner together, and he enjoyed his generous portion of T-bone steak. Since Tina didn't eat red meat, she was happier with chicken or an omelette.

How he managed with so little sleep, Tina didn't know, but the young seem to have unlimited energy when there are exciting things around! Tina had been the same at that age too.

In the apartment complex, there was a large crowd of German tourists. One day, both Tina and Paul were taken aback by one of the lads who was a spitting image of Paul. They could have been twin brothers, such was their likeness! Tina herself mistook the other lad for Paul. She was coming up the steps by the pool with her girlfriend when they spotted the lad sunbathing with a Walkman radio. He was lying on his back, with arms raised above his head. Tina decided to play a prank and went to tickle him under the arm. He sprang up, and Tina was horrified to see that it wasn't Paul after all.

Meanwhile, the lads were eyeing each other, and even got into an odd conversation. Tina then told Paul that very likely the lad was his half-brother, born in Austria, from his dad's days with Helle. One thing was for sure, he was not the one fathered by the chauffeur!

As the saying goes, 'it's a small world' to catch up with one's past actions, and the consequences of them!

Paul had been independent from that time at seventeen,

having his own flat, and working and studying at evening classes. Tina herself had rather flexible working hours, doing shiftwork and every other weekend as well. But this gave her a three-day break the following week. In the summer she could get away to the seaside to Brighton, Eastbourne or Southampton. And once again, she took advantage of being near to the Café de Paris. There she met a few suitable men to go out for dinner dates, but in no time at all they came to the point as to what they had in mind. Within two years she had no less than three propositions put to her to go into a partnership with them!

One of them she had met when working in Bloomsbury, and they had met on and off over the years. His plan was to turn a family business, a former boarding school, into a country club near Oxford.

The second chap was Italian, whom Tina had met years earlier, visiting a nightclub in Soho, where he was a headwaiter. He wanted to branch out, asking her to go into a partnership to open a winebar in Mayfair.

The third chap was a builder and decorator by trade, and he too wanted to start his own business but didn't have enough funds. Tina smelt a rat in every scheme and dropped them from her circle of friends! Still, she was better off than the two dears that she found comparing photographs on a balcony in the Café de Paris, then it dawned on them that they were married to the same bloke. They were so het up by their discovery and determined that he should be charged with bigamy!

50

What Tina has found baffling over the years was the fact that so many people she had encountered socially had formed an impression that she was wealthy. Perhaps it was because she was meant to be, had that unknown criminal not thrown a spanner in the works!

As it was, she was but a working girl, having struggled for so many years until she had saved enough working all hours to keep her head above water.

She went for a breast scan in 1987, and the first examination was clear; but six weeks later she received a letter from the Royal Marsden Hospital to inform her that a closer study of her X-ray showed a cluster of black dots. She was booked as an inpatient for the following week. The waiting time although short, and the four-day stay in the hospital, were very stressful and she feared the worst. Thankfully, the tumours removed from her right breast were not malignant, and she was given the all clear!

She took only one week to convalesce, as living on the premises there wasn't any peace to do so.

Trying to keep her figure in shape, from time to time Tina paid for a gold card that allowed her to use a fitness club at any time of day, whereas she found an annual membership too pricey. She had been working the leg weights, apart from other machines, and didn't feel any strain in her muscles. And yet, for some reason, one day at the office, reaching over from one desk to another her left knee gave out. Soon, the throbbing and swelling started, causing a build-up of inflammation. She was in a great deal of pain with it, but had to wait for an operation for a pulled ligament for eighteen months. Meanwhile, she had treatment at the School of Osteopathy and Physiotherapy, and even a few sessions at a sports injuries clinic at Wellington Hospital, privately.

At the end of a day's work, she didn't know where to put it. Sometimes she held it up on cushions or against a wall, at others she would place a frozen bag of peas on it to cool the inflamed area, and take strong painkillers daily. No high heels either, she got into a habit of wearing trainers going out. Earlier, while she was in the hospital, having the biopsy on her breast, she had a trapped nerve in her neck. It was a similar pain that she had with the knee, and for both of these twice-weekly physiotherapy sessions were a great relief. She finally had an operation, as an inpatient for four days. The night before her release, she made an effort to test her walking. She desperately wanted to go to the bathroom to have a proper wash. Her bed was the last one at the end of the ward, so she was able to lean against it for support.

In the semi-darkness she saw a night nurse, who didn't seem to object to her creeping about. Except, when Tina couldn't get back to her bed she came to her rescue, and only then realised that she shouldn't have got up at all!

The next day the houseman came to see her about it, saying that due to her recovery she might as well go home and use crutches for a while. But Tina declined. Once she was past the pain barrier, she would manage without them. But she promised to attend the physio for a couple of months.

To prove a point, and test her sea-legs, she walked all the way from the hospital on a Friday afternoon. She had to lean on some railings for support and have some rest along the way, but she made it!

On the Monday she was at her desk in the office. The girls were all cock-a-hoop. Where were her crutches, or didn't she have the operation after all? She had to expose her bandaged knee umpteen times!

The pain was bad on some days, and when she went for her consultation she was told that in forcing herself to walk she had done more good than harm. And within a year or so, the knee seemed to have settled back to normal.

Next she had a cyst at the back of her neck. This she had removed under a local anaesthetic at a Harley Street clinic. That same day, she worked a late shift from two to eight p.m. After finishing, she sat down on her sofa, feeling shivers, and noticed a little trickle of discoloured blood running down her neck. She was rather worried, but realised that the clinic would be closed until the next morning. She went to bed, hoping that it would stop.

In the morning she found herself stuck to her pillow by dried blood! she went back to the clinic and had the stitches redone. There was so much pressure that a horrid fluid burst out, like a rainbow!

An infection set in and she had to go there six days a week for a whole month, having it cleansed and the dressing changed. She managed to do her daily hours, as her trips didn't take more than an hour. Still, it was rather a nuisance, having a heavy bandage and restricted movement of her head, and missing her long soak in the bathtub.

She came to the conclusion that going private isn't always the best.

She had two more internal operations, which were carried out at day surgeries. Tina still managed to enjoy her work and contact with the young residents who got up to all sorts of scams, but generally observed the house rules. She remembered one particular incident, when one of the residents received a letter in the morning post. After reading the contents, she appeared rather distressed and ran to the office with it and her prayer-book, asking Tina to take 'a confessional'! She was 'a jack of all trades', but this was out of the question! She advised the girl to go to the nearest Catholic church, as she was of a different denomination in any case.

51

Paul didn't tell Tina about having any serious relationships with girls, but kept busy with his body-building activities. Not until 1990 did he announce that he was in love, and planned to get married when he was twenty-one! She could understand his reasons for wanting to start a family of his own, like Jamie had done at an even younger age. Since their parents had failed dismally in providing a happy home, no doubt both were mature for their years, having to cope independently from a very early age. And thankfully, both were the marrying kind, and made a good job of it, compared to their irresponsible father.

It was time for Tina to buy a hat and attend a church wedding to see her precious son all grown up and getting hitched!

There were five of his mates in top hats and tails in attendance for moral support. Theo was invited, but didn't show, nor did he send a present!

Tina heard on the grapevine that his playboy days had caught up with him. Her prediction on their last meeting had come to pass, that there may come a day when he would find himself wanting!

Having squandered such high earning on women and wine and high living he had become almost a recluse in his retirement. He had lost touch with his friends and was too ashamed to keep in touch with his son and family.

Tina wondered whether he finally felt guilty about the way he had disregarded responsibilities, as any normal husband would have done, from a moral point of view. She found it criminal for any man with means to refuse to provide as a head of the family.

Now he had time to reflect on his actions or lack of them in his loneliness, whereas Tina was happy in gaining a charming and sensible daughter-in-law, and two well-behaved grandchildren by proxy from her previous marriage.

Tina continued to travel further afield. She had met in the course of her work people from all corners of the world and wanted to see the culture and everyday life of various nations.

She travelled to Africa and the Far East. On her visit to Goa, her son and daughter-in-law came along. They had a comfortable villa for a three-week stay. The heat was very intense, day and night. There were no blankets on the beds, and fans were spinning continuously, except during powercuts, which were frequent, but thankfully short-lived. By midday, the sand on the beach got so hot that one couldn't walk on it barefoot!

There were dogs everywhere, running in packs! Not only that, but they were very regimental, each pack observing their borders, lest they got into gang fights. There was one well-fed puppy, but he had a deep gash on his head. Tina felt so sorry for him that she asked one of the gardeners to take him to a vet. He was taken aback by her request, as vets were rather thin on the ground, but Tina was insistent that he find one, and said that she would pay and reward him well for his trouble. They put the puppy into a sack and off they went! In the late afternoon the darling little thing was presented on her veranda, his wound stitched up and covered in flea powder!

From then on, the puppy followed her everywhere, his mother and siblings observing with fascination and suspicion!

At the end of their stay, when she was packing, the puppy was trying to smuggle himself in Tina's suitcase, to go to London.

Animals, wherever they may be, had given her so much pleasure and comfort over the years, more than most people that she has encountered!

A lizard family acted as nightporters, killing insects and flies that were attracted to the wall lighting on their veranda. After sunset, at the same time nightly, they would be flat against the wall clocking in for work punctually! Except for two nights running, they didn't turn up, until the third night, when there appeared thee of them! The parents had brought their offspring to learn the ropes and they were no more than half an inch long!

It was another world out there, as in being back to basics, and one could observe nature at its best and most primitive. There also appeared a cobra, lurking in a coconut tree above the sunbeds around the pool! Once again, nature's creatures gave a signal. A large group of crows in nearby trees shrieked a warning sound and security guards came running from all direction with wooden poles, prepared to deal with a killer reptile!

Paul was scared, although he was over six foot, but managed to get some good photos of it when it was carried away, dead!

Tina escaped tummy upsets and dehydration but got bitten by a poisonous bee during the night. A doctor called to give her injections and a course of antibiotics to help the paralysis to her face muscles.

Along the beachfront, black hogs scavenged among the tourists, and a few oxen joined the crowds on the roads and on the waterfront!

The lifestyle was leisurely and relaxed. Tina and her daughter-in-law, Tessa, even had a hand massage on the sand under a straw roof for shade.

Walking along the narrow roads, they were quite fascinated to see women cooking on open fires and collecting firewood, and even doing heavy work on building sites, breaking stones and fetching and carrying. And from their homesteads, when the front door opened, first trooped out little piglets, chickens and dogs, followed by happy and smiling children.

There was churches everywhere, and the natives, who were of Portuguese origin, observed their religion to the full. Their lifestyle and environment was such an eye-opener and being apart from daily newspapers and television gave one a chance to contemplate the real values of life. Tina found the natives so friendly, and contented with so little material wealth, compared to an affluent society, where greed for even more makes people discontented and stressed. Perhaps there is a middle ground somewhere between these extremes, but Tina had yet to find it.

Her travels in Africa were very revealing in similar ways, but not quite so hot, as the temperature would drop suddenly in the evenings. During one of her Christmas holidays spent in Tunisia, she had yet different experiences.

Although she stayed in a four-star hotel, with well-appointed bedrooms and well cared for gardens, she found the plumbing very primitive. Running a bath, the water first came out rust-coloured, then sandy, and only then some acceptable water! Public toilets she regarded 'no go areas', as the stink would knock one back. Another matter which baffled her was that all the hotel staff were male. Although well-trained and fluent in three languages, her chamberperson kept folding her nightie in so many different ways as if he regarded it as a work of art! She so wanted to use the sauna, but there again the attendant was a man in a long white dress. He set his beady eyes on Tina from top to toe, so she decided it was unwise to strip with him behind the door.

Still, there were compensations, such as ripe oranges falling on her balcony in December and Arabian horses in stables for a good canter!

52

When Tina returned from her vacation in Goa, she learned that her friend and colleague of nine years had given her notice to leave. She could no longer put up with the stress, and left for health reasons. She in fact did most of the interviewing and lettings, and was very highly regarded by the residents, and after her departure, bookings began to drop. The market was there, in fact demand exceeded supply, but for the person in charge it was too much trouble, as she found it easier to leave the beds vacant at the expense of her employers.

Not only that, whenever Tina returned from holidays she had to catch up with a backlog of work for the period that she had been away. To cover the shift of her colleague, the gap was filled by reliefs, who had retired years ago and were able to do only the very basics, such as answer the phone and sort out the post.

The core work fell to Tina, although the old codgers were happy to take a going rate for their wages for a minimum output! Tina sensed, that closure of the hostel was inevitable, long before the head office decided to do just that.

For the second time during her thirty-five-year working career, Tina had witnessed how much damage a wrong person at the helm can inflict on a thriving business!

Had it been someone more competent and public-spirited, the hostel would have remained a happy home for hundreds of young ladies. Tina remained to the very end, to observe the last of the residents move out, with reluctance and sadness. Everyone felt that it was one of the last bastions of value for money housing in central London.

During her years doing temping in West End hotels, Tina experienced a few strange events. In one of them, there was a burst watermain nearby and as a result the water supply was cut off. A tanker pulled into the back entrance to provide an emergency supply. Even the loos had to be flushed with buckets! As the sewage system was practically clear, a water-rat made its way up the loo in a very posh suite! Its occupants, an elderly couple, who were permanent residents, returned to their sitting room only to find a yellow rat playing in their biscuit tin! A night manager managed to kill it, after a lively run around the suite. Inspectors from the Environmental Health made a search of the car park, gardens and drainage. All were satisfactory, and their conclusion was that the creature was a one-off intruder, although a fearsome looking one at that!

In another hotel there were some five hundred bedrooms, plus a hundred apartments next door, and a total of six telephones in the housekeeping office. Tina was the first one in the office that morning, and answered one of them. On the line there was a woman screaming that her husband was having a heart attack!

Tina located their room on the fourth floor, where a young mother was trying to bottlefeed a screaming infant, while the husband, not more than forty, was going blue in the face, lying on the floor!

Tina loosed his tie and collar while she worked on getting some air to his lungs. Seemingly, they had overslept, and the husband had panicked about missing a very important appointment. Well, he missed it anyway, but the main thing was that he lived!

And in yet another, a tourist who had drunk more than his fair share was beheaded by leaning over a lift shaft! Thankfully, she didn't witness the incident, but saw the telltale bloodstains on a light-coloured carpet by the lift. Something so gory doesn't bear thinking about, but should make everyone aware of the health and safety regulations, when it comes to elevators.

In a hotel in north London, one guest was rather an oddball. He only stayed for two hours, after booking in for the night. The following morning, one of the maids asked Tina to come and see the havoc in one of the suites. A beautiful set of silk curtains had been ripped off their brass railings, and dumped into a bathtub, where the shower curtains had suffered the same fate! The glass of an antique mirror was cracked, having had an Oriental vase thrown at it! But the strangest find was a plastic carrier bag containing £700 in cash and a room key to one of the well-known hotels in Park Lane!

Tina found out from the night manager, who had booked him in around eleven p.m. the previous evening, that the man had seemed very nervous, but was smartly dressed. On leaving the hotel two hours later, with a bleeding hand, he had informed the nightman that he couldn't stay because there was someone in his room persecuting him! He figured that the guest was high on drugs, hence such havoc left behind. The man was never traced, as he had paid in cash and the best thing was the moneybag left behind to cover for the damage.

53

This time around, Tina settled happily in her new flat, appreciating her privacy, and glad to be away from it all! She no longer felt isolated and on her leisurely walks along the footpaths of the River Thames she had a chance to reflect on life's trials and tribulations.

When still at college, she enrolled for a short course in physiology. One of the lectures and a discussion to follow was about a 'war-child'. They talked about the children born during the war years and how the fear and stress of a situation for expectant mothers affected their children and could lead to depression and suicide when reaching their teens. Tina was aware of a few cases among her fellow students, however the numbers were minimal taking the population of the whole country into account, being only four-and-a-half million.

Did the war years affect her? Surely, but in channelling her thoughts to positive thinking.

A lot has changed in the past thirty years since Tina's fateful journey on that Russian liner. Since president J.F. Kennedy, there had been a number of presidents in the United States of America and the same applied to Russia. Margaret Thatcher had a good innings in bringing the two enemy nations to a handshake, and peaceful cooperation. To have their activities in the open, the Berlin Wall had come down, and so had the Iron Curtain.

Regardless, the devil continued to be a busy man, as Fabian had put it! And it was very unlikely that either MI5 or the KGB would ever be out of work.

Such is man's greed for power and bloodshed that there is a war going on somewhere in the world all the time, although on a smaller scale. One doesn't have to look very far to be aware of such activities in media coverage: Eastern Europe, Asia, the Middle East and Africa.

The difference for the fighting and killing is even stranger, in that it is often internal within a country on religious or economic grounds. In Africa it is between different tribes, based on tyranny and money.

If the wars didn't continue to kill populations *en masse*, would the planet become overpopulated? Or would natural disasters, such as famine, floods and epidemics be enough?

Perhaps not. Human nature appears to be focused on high drama or simply a winning situation!

There has yet to be born a leader, be it a man or woman, who can keep all the warring nations on an even keel. Then again, should our lives be all plain sailing, then surely the joy of living would lose its charm?

Still, Tina wondered what the future would hold for her two lovely granddaughters, Melody and Melissa. Melody had already appeared in a TV advert, and was a natural for posing in front of cameras. Perhaps her path would lead to Hollywood, whereas granny only got as far as a West End club!

Whenever Tina saw an impressive white mansion with verandas she could not help asking, 'Who lives in one like that in Devon?' They do say that all wrongdoers get their comeuppance sooner or later, so there is hope that one in particular has already met his Waterloo.